Let's Pretend
We Never
Met

Also by Melissa Walker

Why Can't I Be You

Let's Pretend We Never Met

Melissa Walker

HARPER

An Imprint of HarperCollinsPublishers

Library of Congress Control Number: 2016961161
ISBN 978-0-06-256717-8

Typography by Alison Klapthor
18 19 20 CG/BRR 10 9 8 7 6 5 4 3 2 1
❖
First paperback edition, 2018

For Ida Lou, my newest love

Chapter 1

When Mama and Daddy sat me down to tell me that my grandmother in Philadelphia needed our help, that she was getting older and wanted to see us more, I knew what they were doing.

They were making it so that if I refused to go, if I kicked and screamed like they knew I would, I'd look selfish, like a spoiled eleven-year-old who doesn't care about her poor, frail grandmother.

The truth is, I love my grandmother (I call her by her first name, Maeve) because she lets me borrow ivory-colored combs for my hair and doesn't mind when I open up her "traveling trunk" and dig through it to pick out silk scarves to spin around in.

I am an excellent granddaughter.

But leaving in the *middle* of sixth grade? Not even at the start of a school year? Right before Isabel Jessup's twelfth birthday party, where she's going to have a chocolate fountain? This is unfair. Unreasonable. Outrageous.

I argued until I heard Daddy say my full name: "Mathilda Maeve Markham!" And then I knew: that was that.

I wish I had a sibling so we could at least team up. The biggest protest I can think of is riding in the way-wayback of our minivan with my arms crossed over my chest as we drive from North Carolina, which takes like nine hours. That's nine hours of Mama and Daddy knowing that I'm *angry* and I don't want to go.

But after an hour, I fall asleep against the window, and when I wake up I'm hungry and Mama offers to stop at Burger King, so I get a cheeseburger and move to the middle row of seats, because they're more comfortable for eating. Besides, it was getting lonely in the way-wayback.

"We're going to be on the top floor of an apartment

building," says Mama. She's told me this at least ten times, but it's one of the things I'm sort of excited about. Apartment buildings are fancy.

"Tell me about the door guy again," I say.

"Door*man*," says Daddy. "There are a few of them, but I met a nice one named Will."

"And he wears a uniform?" I've been told this is the case, but I want to confirm it. It's another thing I'm sort of excited about. We don't have uniformed doormen in my town in North Carolina.

"He does indeed. Black with brass buttons."

I sit back in my seat and look out the window. It might be like having a butler, which I've only seen in movies.

As I watch the highway miles go by, the green ground turns white with the frost of December snow up north, and the restaurants change from Hardee's to Roy Rogers. I wonder what else might be different about this move. Will *I* be different? *Can* I?

At my old school, I played it safe. I was in the middle— not the smartest kid or the one with the most friends, but not at the bottom. Maybe this is my chance to move up.

★ ★ ★

We stop at my grandmother's house for the night before we go on to our new apartment—the moving van isn't coming until tomorrow, so we wouldn't have beds to sleep in yet.

When Maeve's tall, thin shadow steps into the entryway light, I smile and rush forward for a hug. She smells like Shalimar, a perfume she bought in France. Like travel and romance.

My grandfather died before I was born, so Maeve is alone in this big, old row house in the middle of the city. It's got three floors and it's really narrow, and I always thought it would make a great movie-set house because it has polished wood floors and real built-in fireplaces—not to mention a stained-glass bay window in the living room and a creepy old basement covered in dust.

"Your bed's all ready, Honeypie," Maeve says. If anyone else called me that I'd probably make a face, but Maeve has nicknames for us all, and she grew up in West Virginia, so her voice is soft and sweet and southern and her *Honeypie* sounds like whispered love.

When she tucks me in a few minutes later, she brushes

the hair off my forehead and says, "It's hard to move to a new place, isn't it?"

I nod, but my eyes are half-closed, I'm already drifting away, into the soft, feathery comforter that floats around me like a cloud.

"Don't worry, Honeypie." Her voice is soothing. "You're sweeter than peach cobbler, and prettier than a bluebird."

I don't believe her—she's my *grandmother*, after all—but I fall asleep smiling anyway. Because when I'm with Maeve, I'm home. For one more night anyway.

Chapter 2

When I start unpacking, it really hits me: I live here now. My purple-painted room with the light-green carpet and the white lace curtains that would never fit these big apartment windows? Gone. Not mine. Some other kid is at my old window, looking out at the dogwood tree and listening to the whippoorwill sing.

That is so weird. I know it's not very nice of me, but I don't think I like that new kid.

I wonder if a kid was in *this* room before me. Maybe they're even missing it right now, like I'm missing my old room. I haven't figured out what's special about this apartment yet, but I'm sure something is. When you live somewhere you find all kinds of reasons to get attached to a place.

In our house in North Carolina, there was a little closet under the stairs that had a slanted ceiling. I had a lamp in there that spun in a circle and lit up the walls with blue stars. When I was younger, it was the perfect place for tea parties, and when I outgrew those it was for secret-telling when my best friends Lily and Josephine came over. I have to find a safe whisper spot in this apartment, once I make some friends.

The view outside my window is not of city lights, which is what I imagined I'd see here. There's actually another building really close to ours, so although I get some light from above, there's mainly a brick wall in front of my face when I look outside. Mama frowned when she opened up my blinds and realized that—Daddy found the apartment, so she hadn't ever seen it—but I told her it made me feel like a city kid, which is cool.

There's a mirror on one wall that was here when we arrived. It has a dark wood frame and it's hung right at my height. I give my reflection a once-over and pull out my ponytail, letting my long brown hair fall down to the middle of my back. It's slightly curly in a way that can either look messy or cute, depending on the weather, and I decide that I'm going to wear it down on the first day of school after winter break. I know that the first time kids see you, they decide things about you, and I want to be a girl with long hair.

I hear Mama's cell phone ring, and I stay still to listen. Our regular phone isn't set up yet, and my parents are cave people who won't get me a cell, so . . .

"Mattie!"

Yes!

Mama brings me the phone. "It's Lily," she says.

I squeal and grab it.

"Lils!"

"Mat!"

"What's up? Has Ryan texted you yet?"

Lily gave her number to Ryan Grant at a last-day-before-break holiday party, which is pretty much the same as becoming his girlfriend. We *think*.

"Not yet, but Jo and I think he'll probably text me either on Christmas Day or the day after, so we can talk about what we got and we won't have to wonder what to say."

Her voice is bubbly and excited, but my heart stings when she says *Jo and I think* because I already feel like they're forgetting me. I've always been closer to Lily than Josephine, like it was the two of us plus Jo . . . but now that's different.

I act happy, though. No one wants a downer who moved away as a friend.

"That's so true!" I say. "He probably wants to be sure y'all will have a lot to talk about."

"Exactly," says Lily. "And Jo also thinks that he's going to ask me to a movie. I'll definitely say yes but haven't decided if I'm going to let him kiss me or not."

Whoa. "Kiss you?" I ask, and she must hear the surprise in my voice.

"Yeah!" says Lily. "We're not babies anymore, Mattie. Jo and I think we should try to get our first kiss this year. We're almost *twelve*."

"Oh," I say, hesitating. "Good idea."

Lily laughs. "I forgot that you don't know anyone yet!

Oh, but Mattie, that could be so exciting. New *boys*!"

"I know," I say, trying to sound upbeat but not really sure how I feel about all the *new* in my life.

"Jo and I think that you might really blossom this year," says Lily, sounding like a doctor or something.

"What does *that* mean?" I ask.

"I don't know, just that you've always been quiet and stuff," she says. "Maybe you'll have more fun at your new school."

More fun? "I think we have fun," I say to her.

"We did!" says Lily, and then she corrects herself. "We do! Oh, forget I said that. Maybe I said it wrong. Gah!"

I can almost see her stick her tongue out over the phone. Lily does sometimes say things in a weird way.

"It's okay," I say, trying to ignore the heaviness that's settling into my chest. "Yeah, I'm going to try to make this year a lot of fun."

Lily tells me that her mom keeps talking about missing my mom because she really wants Mama's magic bars at the school's holiday bake sale, and then she has to go because her dad wants her help wrapping presents.

When we hang up, my room feels even more empty. I didn't realize my best friends thought of me as "the quiet one." Maybe I don't say much out loud, but inside I'm full of fun ideas and random thoughts. I thought they knew that. I thought they knew me.

Chapter 3

I frown at the white walls of my bedroom. I'm mostly unpacked and I'm holding my star lamp but I'm not sure it'll feel right in here. I wish this room had more personality. It's so . . . blank. I don't want to be blank, and I don't want my room to be either.

Maybe they paint everything back-to-boring white when new people move in. I sit down on the floor and scratch my fingernail against the wall behind my bed. It takes some doing, but once I get through a layer of paint, I see that there's a pale orange underneath the white.

Huh. That's kind of cool. I don't know if it's a boy color or a girl color, but I decide that the kid here before me had style. Or at least a "sense of self," which my dad always says I have. It's a good thing, having a sense of self. It means I'm going to paint these walls, or maybe even get wallpaper, very soon.

We're on the ninth floor, which is the very top of Butler Towers. They aren't actually that tall, as tall buildings go, but I've only lived in a two-story house before, so we seem way high up to me. Our town is outside of Philadelphia, in the suburbs. When Dad first said we were moving here, I pictured Maeve's neighborhood—which has rows of houses stuck together along a cobblestone street. And then when he said we'd be living in an apartment building, I imagined downtown, with skyscrapers and train stations. This town is not as cool as all that—it's kind of like my town in North Carolina—but Dad was right about the doormen: they do wear brass buttons. Plus, there's an elevator. I love the elevator.

"Mattie?"

Mama's in her room. We will never have to raise our voices in this apartment, because there are just two bedrooms and they're both right next to the living room, which is right next to the kitchen.

"Mama?"

She walks into the hallway, brushing dusty hands on her jeans. Her nails are short and her dark-red polish is chipped, which is unlike her. She's usually very put together, but right now she's doing all the unpacking since Daddy is over at Maeve's house helping out.

Daddy already has a job—he starts at a law firm on Monday—and Mama's been looking for work, but so far she hasn't found anything. I'm not worried, though; I know she will. She ran the bakery at a restaurant in North Carolina, and she always says she's happiest when she's baking; she makes the very best cakes and cookies I've ever tasted, including the kinds you buy from fancy places. And I don't think that just because she's my mama. I mean, Lily's mom is still talking about the magic bars.

I heard my parents arguing last night. Mama was saying something about Maeve. I know because Mama said, "She's *your* mother." Then today when Daddy left the house, Mama gestured to all the boxes and gave him a look and Daddy said, "Well, you wanted me to talk to her!"

When my parents argue, Mama's voice gets really high

and tight, but Daddy always sounds calm. It makes him seem like he's winning, so I've tried to take note of that and use it in my own arguments. Not that I've had many. Still, the low-talking technique is in my back pocket if I need it.

"Want some help in here?" Mama stands in my doorway.

I scoot away from the scratches I made on the wall and make sure my comforter falls into place to cover them.

"Sure." I start to open one of the three boxes left. It's marked "Mattie Dresser."

For the next hour, Mama helps me put my clothes away and reassemble my bookshelf, but when we come to the very last box, a tiny one that has silver duct tape all around the edges, I tell her I want to finish up myself. This is the box that I sealed at the very end, the night before we drove away from North Carolina forever. This box has the Good Stuff.

"Okay, Mattie, my dear," Mama says, tousling my hair. "I'll make us a snack."

I wait until she walks out and then I close the door and sit on the bed with my box. I shut my eyes and think about each of the three things inside.

First, there's the piece of paper where I played MASH for the last time with Lily and Josephine. MASH is a game where you learn your future, and in this round I got the very best possible outcome: I'm famous and living in a mansion with Josh Jensen and we have two kids and drive a BMW.

Second is a piece of fool's gold that Daddy and I found in our driveway two summers ago. It's not your ordinary fool's gold—it's a *giant* chunk with five smooth sides and one rough edge. I saw it glinting in the sunlight and thought someone had dropped a locket or something . . . it's that big. I wonder if they have fool's gold in Pennsylvania, but then I remember that I don't have a driveway anymore, so where would I look for it?

And third: the ring. It's not a silver ring or something with a sparkly gemstone or anything—it's much more than that. It's a piece of twine tied into a bow. Josh Jensen gave it to me at sleepaway camp last summer. I mean, he sort of did. We were in the craft hut during free hour one day, and I was making friendship bracelets while he practiced his sailing knots on the other side of the room.

He was completely ignoring me, not even looking up, but then—right when the brass bell called us for dinner—he came over and laid the ring on the table in front of me, saying, "Here."

It was the greatest thing a boy's ever said to me.

I didn't even like Josh Jensen as anything more than a guy from camp, but suddenly he became *Josh Jensen*. The twine stayed tied too, right in a neat bow that fits perfectly on my fourth finger. I wish he knew that I wear it whenever I'm nervous, that it's going to help me through my first day at a new school after winter break. If my parents would let me get any kind of online account besides plain old email I could show him.

I use scissors to get through the tape. Then I open the box and take out my three treasures. When I look at them plainly, they don't seem very special—a piece of folded paper, a rock, and some string. But when I line them up on my windowsill overlooking the parking lot, they make the room feel like home, and I'm more at ease.

At least until I hear the banging from next door.

Chapter 4

"I'm Agnes P. Davis," says the brown-eyed girl with pale skin and boy-short blond hair who opens the door to 914 Butler Towers when Mama and I knock.

We didn't even have a chance to ask.

"Hi, Agnes," says Mama. "I'm Mrs. Markham, and this is my daughter, Mattie."

"You look my age," Agnes says to me. "I'm eleven years, two months, and four days."

She stares at me expectantly.

"I'm, uh . . ." I try to do some math in my head, but who can think so fast? "I'm eleven too," I say.

"You sound like a country singer," she says to me.

"I'm from North Carolina," I tell her, nervous that she'll make fun of me. Lily and Josephine told me that people up north are sometimes mean about accents. *They'll tell you you sound stupid*, they said.

But Agnes P. Davis just says, "Cool!" And she grabs my hand. "Let's play!"

None of my friends at home still *play*. We hang out, we talk, we do stuff. Before I have time to react, she jerks me inside her apartment. I look back at Mama with wide eyes, but she just smiles and peeks her head in, looking for the parents of Agnes P. Davis.

"Mrs. Davis? Mr. Davis? We heard some banging. . . ." I hear Mama calling as I zoom past a neatly organized living room and into a bedroom of crazy.

The first things I see are the walls. One striped, one polka-dotted, one with stars, and one with tall flowers painted on it. I cannot even list all the colors, but believe me, the rainbow is here. And when this girl said *play*, she meant it. There are Bratz dolls, Care Bears, and My Little Ponies all over this room. At first it looks chaotic, but when my eyes settle among the bouncing patterns, I see that all of the toys are carefully lined up on shelves and in baskets.

"Wow. This is . . . ," I start.

"Don't you love it?" she says, her smile taking up almost her whole face. "I'm into colors and shapes and numbers, and I think everything should have its own space and place so that the world can be an ordered collection of magic and wonder. That's my design philosophy. What's yours?"

"Um . . ." Agnes P. Davis makes me not able to talk. *Design philosophy?*

"What's your room like?" she asks.

"Well, it's not really set up yet, so . . ."

Zooooom. Agnes P. Davis is out of here, heading for our apartment's open door.

I follow her, passing a bewildered Mama, who apparently can't find the parents of our kooky neighbor.

"Agnes, honey, where's your mama?" she asks, after we get back to our own apartment, where Agnes is standing in the smack-dab middle of my bedroom.

"She's grocery shopping," says Agnes.

"And your daddy?"

"In Boston." Agnes puts one hand under her chin and

tilts her head sideways as she stares at my white walls.

"Blue swirls here," she says, turning to me. "You look like a swirly girl."

I look to Mama to explain this hurricane that just blew into our apartment.

"Do you want to stay awhile, Agnes?" she asks.

I freeze. That's my line. If someone is my age, I'm the one who gets to invite them over. Mama should know that. But then I remember that Agnes is already here, so maybe it doesn't matter.

"I have to!" replies Agnes. "You closed my door, right?"

Mama nods slowly.

"It auto-locks, and I don't have the keys with me."

"Oh," says Mama. "I'll leave a note on the door for your mother, then."

"Thanks!" Agnes smiles that big smile again. "She'll be home by seven-oh-four p.m."

Then she lies across my double bed, staring at the ceiling with her arms behind her head. "I think glow-in-the-dark stars will look great up there," she says. She flops over onto her stomach. "So swirls on that wall, stars above . . . what other ideas do you have?"

Mama gives me a grin as she leaves the room, and I am alone with the craziest girl I've ever met.

I circle the bed slowly, unsure whether to sit down with Agnes or not. Suddenly my white-walled room feels like it's pulsing with color.

"The kid before me had the walls painted orange," I say, leaning down to show her the spot where I scratched away the white. "Did you know him? Or her?"

She hangs her body half off the bed, legs in the air as she twists to peek behind the comforter.

"No," she says. "This apartment's been empty since we got here, but I can tell that whoever it was is a big thinker. Orange is the color of misunderstood genius."

Then she pops up. "Sorry about the banging, by the way," she says. "From now on we'll have a quieter signal—I'll shine a light outside my room onto that wall." She points to the brick in front of my window.

And before I can ask her what she means, I see her eyes lock on the windowsill. It makes me nervous, the way she stops talking when she sees what's sitting up there.

She stands and walks over to my objects, and it's the slowest her muscles have moved since I met her. She bends over and holds her face very close to each one—the folded paper, the fool's gold, and the twine ring—without touching anything.

Then she straightens. She looks back at me with knowing eyes.

"Your treasures."

I nod, and she mirrors me.

"I have some too," she says.

Chapter 5

Christmas Day at Maeve's is one of my favorite things—we usually come up to Philadelphia from North Carolina, but now that we live here, it's a ten-minute ride. On the drive over, Mama talks about how pretty the old stone houses are, and Daddy points out where some of his friends from growing up used to live. "Do you still know any of your friends from back then?" I ask, but Daddy shakes his head and says he's lost touch with them.

My parents met in college down south, and they stayed in the same town Mama grew up in. Daddy always says he got the hometown beauty queen because one time Mama was chosen to wave from the top of a float during a town parade. My first-grade teacher, Ms. Gray, was her first-grade teacher too! But now all that sameness is gone because Mama's never lived up here. She's also never not had a job, at least as far back as I can remember. It already seems weird that she's been home during the day, even though she goes online every afternoon looking for openings at restaurants and bakeries nearby. But it's given us a chance to unpack—and for her to bake at home. She's bringing enough cookies to feed fifty people over to Maeve's today.

My cousin Elodie and her parents, Uncle Jay and Aunt Cindy, drove down from Vermont. After we all greet one another, my dad and her dad—the brothers—tell stories while Elodie and I sit on the red Persian rug in the living room.

We don't watch television at Maeve's. She has a big, boxy TV upstairs, but it just doesn't seem like the thing to do here, so we stay downstairs and listen to the sound of our fathers' voices while our mothers help Maeve in the kitchen. I always think it seems like something people in olden times would do—gather in a room and tell stories without TV on or anything. Daddy brought his iPad over, but we don't swipe it on even once.

"Tell me again why you're not staying in the extra bedrooms here? There's plenty of room, and you could save money. Plus, you might get the sale done a lot quicker." Aunt Cindy says this to Mama as they deliver drinks to us (something clear with ice for my dad and Uncle Jay; Shirley Temples with bright-red cherries for me and Elodie).

"The sale?" asks Elodie.

"Because I don't want everyone in my business," says Maeve from behind them, cutting off the conversation as she carries in a tray of cheese and nuts. She sets it down on the marble-top coffee table near me, and Elodie and I each reach for a slice of cheddar.

"I'm perfectly capable of caring for myself." Maeve smiles at my dad. "It's just nice to have some kin nearby."

The three of them go back into the kitchen, and I see Aunt Cindy shoot Uncle Jay a smile as she walks out of the room. He winks back. I wonder if they thought about moving closer to Maeve, or if it was always going to be us.

After a story that I love even though I've heard it a hundred times—about a bullying neighbor who swung her roller skates at Uncle Jay and then got hers when Daddy set up a trip wire near her front door—Mama comes in and gives Daddy a look, no smile.

"What?" he asks.

"Your mother would like some help in the kitchen," she says.

"Isn't that what *you're* doing?" Daddy laughs, looking at Uncle Jay instead of at Mama, who folds her arms across her chest and lets out a deep breath. She spins and walks out, but Daddy follows her, saying, "Liz, I'm just kidding. Don't be so uptight."

Uncle Jay ruffles Elodie's curly blond hair and says, "I'm gonna run to the loo."

That means the bathroom. Uncle Jay is always saying things in a foreign way. Daddy says it's because he lived in England. Mama says it's because he's snobby.

I wonder if Uncle Jay and Aunt Cindy ever get snippy with each other like Mama and Daddy have been doing lately. I've never seen it, but Mama says you don't know what happens behind closed doors and all families have their issues.

"I'm getting an e-reader for Christmas," Elodie tells

me when we're alone in the living room.

"You already know your presents?"

She shrugs. "Some of them."

I don't think it's very fun to know what you're going to unwrap on Christmas Day, but Elodie has always been practical. She has a way of saying things that makes them seem simple and also true.

Elodie points to her e-reader. She even knows which box it's in. All of my gifts, wrapped in the same blue-and-gold drummer-boy paper, are going to be a surprise.

There are felt ornaments on the tree that Maeve's neighbor sewed over lots of years—a light-blue Volkswagen Bug car that looks like one Maeve drove in with my grandfather across the country in the 1960s; a camel with silver sequin eyes as a reminder of a trip to Morocco; a unicorn with white fringe for a mane and tail because there's a unicorn tapestry in New York City that Maeve loves and always talks about taking me to see. Everything in this house has a story. I let my vision go fuzzy at the glow of the multicolored lights among the green branches.

"I have one more week before school," I tell Elodie. She's a year older than I am, so maybe she has some advice.

"Me too," she says.

"Yeah, but I'm gonna be at a new school with all new kids."

"Oh, right," she says. "That'll be awkward."

So much for the wisdom of older cousins.

The crystal dinner bell tinkles.

Elodie and I jump up quickly. The dining room is warm and full of goodness; there's a turkey just out of the oven, and the air is thick with the smell of delicious gravy. The table is set with the nice china—white with gold edges and a tiny pink rose pattern—and the sight of the food makes my stomach growl: homemade stuffing with croutons and raisins; a heaping bowl of mashed potatoes dotted with melting butter; long, stringy green beans with bacon fat; and a bowl of cranberry sauce still shaped like the can because Maeve thinks that's better than homemade, and I do too.

Daddy's bringing out glasses of water for everyone, and I watch him bump Mama's hip when he passes her. She tries not to smile, but I see a hidden grin when he whispers, "See, I'm helping."

What we're all really focused on, though, is the

silverware. A long time ago, one of the knives went into the oven accidentally. Part of the metal melted and dropped into the hollow handle, so now if you shake the knife, it rattles. When Maeve sets the table she decides who gets the musical knife—it's a big honor.

I told Agnes P. Davis about the knife and she understood instantly. Before we left for Maeve's, we saw her and her mom in the hallway and instead of "Merry Christmas" she said, "Have a rattle-ful day!" I noticed her apartment door was completely covered in wrapping paper with a big bow crossed over it, like it was a present.

When everyone is in their usual seats, we bow our heads in thanks. We're not religious, but we're grateful on holidays.

"We thank you for the food we are about to eat, and for the company we keep," says Uncle Jay. "We're thankful for many years of Christmases in this house, and for this final holiday here."

My eyes fly open and so do Elodie's.

"What?!" we say in unison.

Maeve's hand squeezes mine. "We'll talk about it later,

Honeypie," she says. Then I see her throw Uncle Jay a mad look.

I glance at my mother, who nods. "Don't worry, Mattie. Maeve may not want to keep hosting holidays and—"

Maeve's voice is loud as she interrupts Mama and says, "Well, now, no one's even reached for their knife yet!" And Daddy says, "Amen!"

An uneasy feeling settles into my chest, but everyone else starts picking up their silverware, so I grab my own knife and shake.

It rattles!

"Mattie got the musical knife!" says Uncle Jay.

"You know that means you're going to have good luck all next year," says Daddy.

I smile and I feel my face flush with pleasure as I relax into my seat. Everything will be okay. When I look over at Maeve gratefully, she wiggles her eyebrows at me. I'm going to need all the lucky knife moments I can get.

Chapter 6

The best gifts I got for Christmas were in my stocking. Weird, I know. One was a package of glow-in-the-dark stars, and the other was a gift certificate to Home Depot.

"I guess Santa thinks you might want to set up your room," said Mama. I knew she was thinking of the day we met Agnes P. Davis and I started considering my design philosophy.

Mama talked to Mrs. Davis that night, and she found out that Agnes's mom is a really important person at a new start-up—she works long hours. Mr. Davis is still back in Boston, where they moved from in the fall. When my mom offered to keep an eye on both of us during this winter break, Mrs. Davis said she thought Agnes was old enough to stay home alone, and my mom said that was probably true but that she'd be happy to have Agnes come over whenever she liked. I saw Mrs. Davis smile at that, and I can tell she's glad we live next door.

"Mattie, I think Agnes has been alone a lot," Mama told me one night when she was tucking me into bed.

"Then it's good we moved in, right?" I said, and Mama smiled and told me I was a kind soul.

It's only been a week of us living here, but Agnes is at my apartment every day now. She knocks in the morning, and she goes home for dinner when her mom gets back from work. Mrs. Davis has dark curly hair and friendly brown eyes under round red-rimmed glasses—she looks like one of the nurses at my old school. She seems a lot calmer than Agnes, so I bet Agnes's father is the one with all the crazy parts.

I'm starting to like the crazy parts, though.

Agnes is never bored, which means I am never bored when I'm with her. Here is what we like to do:

1. *Ride up and down in the elevators. When people get in, we*

call each other by fake names and pretend to be who we're not. Once she pretended to be a boy named Steven, which made me snort-laugh into the back of my sleeve.

2. Talk to the doormen. I think Agnes's mom has a deal with them or something, because Will knocks on her door every morning to deliver an egg sandwich, and someone who's on duty comes up to check on her a few times a day. Agnes says the doormen have a lot of thoughts to share—she made friends with them way back when she moved in at the end of the summer, and they liked me immediately too. They told me that any friend of Agnes's is a friend of theirs, which I've heard people say on TV but never in real life. When I'm talking to the doormen, it feels like I'm an important person. Our favorites are Will and Jessica, who say they should be called doorpeople, and I know that's true, but I just don't think that word has the same ring to it.

3. Cook. Agnes's mom has these chef cards from TV that are all three-ingredient recipes. That means they're easy enough for kids to make. Agnes has me prep the ingredients, and then she mixes and does all the cooking work. That's fine with me, because I don't really like the open-flame situation we have now—in North Carolina we had an electric stove top, which

was much less scary. *Nothing we've made has tasted good yet, but Agnes says it doesn't matter, that it's about our "process." And I'm into chopping things.*

Mama likes having Agnes around too—I can tell. She left us alone for two hours once when she went out to pick up job applications at cafés and bakeries in the city, but mostly she's been hanging out at home with us. Daddy is busy with his new job, and I guess Maeve really did need us here, because he's stopped by her house almost every night after work this week. He hasn't been getting home until after I go to bed.

Tonight is New Year's Eve, though, and Daddy has the day off. He and Mama are going to a fancy party at his boss's house, and he's gone to pick up Maeve and bring her over to stay with me. Maeve hasn't had a license since 1981, when she was just learning to drive and she was in an accident where Uncle Jay's arm got broken. "I'm a city girl and I'll stick to the train, thank you," she says, if anyone asks her about it.

I'm setting up two decks of cards for a game of Double Solitaire, Maeve's favorite, when I hear a rapid knock that could only be Agnes P. Davis at the door.

"Hi!" She walks right in and sits at the table in front of one of the decks. "What are we playing?"

"My grandmother Maeve is coming over," I tell her. "We play Double Solitaire."

Agnes scrunches up her face and looks at me funny. "Is that possible?" she asks.

"Of course."

"Doesn't *solitaire* mean *alone*? As in you're playing a game by yourself?"

I never thought about that. Agnes makes me think about lots of things I never thought about before.

"Where's my Honeypie?" Maeve's sweet voice sends me running to the door, and I give her a big hug. I love the feel of her soft cashmere sweater on my face. She kisses the top of my head and asks, "Who's this now?"

I turn to see Agnes staring at Maeve.

"Maeve, this is Agnes P. Davis," I say. "She lives next door."

"Hello, Lightning Bug," says Maeve.

Agnes tilts her head really far sideways. "Why did you call me that?"

"It just came to me," says Maeve. "I see who you are, and I *appreciate* you as the little lightning bug glowing in front of me."

I look at Agnes anxiously, wondering if Maeve's habit of giving people nicknames the moment she meets them is going to make her upset.

But Agnes smiles and says, "I like fireflies." Then she bolts into the dining room and yells, "Double Solitaire is all set up, Grandmother Maeve!"

"You can leave out the *grandmother* part!" Maeve laughs as I take her hand and pull her into the apartment. She looks at the table. "Let's get another deck of cards, Honeypie," she says to me. "What we have here is a game of *Triple* Solitaire!"

The three of us play a few rounds, but Maeve keeps putting the clubs on the spades and the hearts on the dia-monds. I tell her to stop cheating, and she tells me to stop sassing her. And even though Agnes claims she's never heard of this game before, she's very good at it. She wins twice, and Maeve says it's all in the speed of her lightning bug hands. That makes Agnes beam.

"I like your bracelet, Maeve," says Agnes, and I look to

see the gold cuff flashing in the light as my grandmother makes her moves.

"Thank you, Agnes. It's part of a series that was made by a local artist in the early twentieth century."

"I know," says Agnes. "I saw others like it at the Germantown Historical Society."

"What a culture bug you are—that's a lovely place!" says Maeve, and while they're talking museums I get a few more cards out into the middle. I think I'm going to win this round. "They have histories of important neighborhood residents, Mattie," says Maeve, and I nod without really listening as she goes on about how beautiful the collection is.

"I liked the story of the lady with the parrot," says Agnes.

"It was a cockatoo," says Maeve. "They can live eighty years or more, and she had to will it to her children."

Agnes laughs.

"The historical society has a real archive of the area closest to my heart," my grandmother says.

Agnes nods up and down, up and down, and even though she's in a conversation, her hands are still faster than mine. She wins again.

Mama and Daddy get dressed to leave, and when they come out of their bedroom, they look like famous people. Daddy's wearing a black tuxedo, and he has sparkling studs at the end of his sleeves—cuff links, Maeve calls them. Mama's in a red dress with a really low back. The skirt goes all the way to the ground.

"You look like a smooth glass of poured cherry liqueur," Maeve tells her.

Mama did her own manicure this morning and her nails are painted a shiny dark gray that looks good with her dress and her hair is curled at the ends. I asked her why she wasn't going to a salon like she usually did when she had a fancy night planned, and she said, "Not until I find a job," but I think she did great at home, and I can't even tell the difference.

"You look so pretty, Mama," I say.

Agnes P. Davis just lets out a long, low whistle, which makes us all laugh—even Daddy.

Maeve says I can stay up until midnight, but Agnes goes home at nine, after her mom knocks. When she leaves she says, "Wait for my signal," and then disappears out the door before I can ask what that means. I try to stay awake watching the celebrities and the musical performances on TV, but I fall asleep on the couch, so Maeve wakes me up and walks me to my room, where she lets me go to bed in my clothes.

"You're sleepier than a rag doll without a bone in her body, Honeypie," Maeve whispers, and I fall asleep again before she even clicks out my light.

Bangbangbang.

I wake up to a knock on my wall and roll over to look at the clock. 11:47 p.m.

Bangbangbang.

The signal. I thought Agnes said it would be quieter.

If Mama and Daddy would let me have a cell phone, I could call Agnes right now—she, like every other eleven-year-old I know, has one. Mama told me that's because her mom works late sometimes and likes to check in. I told Mama she could feel free to work late at whatever new job she finds, but she swatted me on the behind and told me not to be fresh.

I sit up in bed and realize that there's a light shining on the brick wall outside my window. When I look closer, I see that it's in the shape of a star, and it seems like it's coming from Agnes P. Davis's room. *Cool.* This is definitely the signal.

I tiptoe into the living room. The TV is on and a glittering ball is behind a big countdown clock that has eleven minutes left on it. Maeve is asleep on the couch, her head propped up on a throw pillow. I smile. Even grown-ups can't stay awake for New Year's Eve.

Moving quietly, I walk to the front door and undo the two locks very slowly so they don't click too loudly.

When I peek out into the hallway, Agnes P. Davis's face pops up in front of me.

"Hi!" She points a flashlight at me, and I see she taped custom-cut black construction paper over it so that it shines in the shape of a star.

"I love that," I tell her, and she reminds me that beaming a light on the outside wall is our secret signal if we ever need each other. "Like a lighthouse in a storm," she says. "But I had to knock this time too, because you didn't come out fast enough!"

"I fell asleep!"

"That's okay," she says. Then she hands me a cone-shaped birthday hat. "Come sit."

"In the hall?"

"Of course." She drops to the floor, stretching her legs out on the hall carpet and leaning up against the wall. She's wearing a clunky watch on her wrist, and she has on a party hat too. There's a big canvas bag next to her with a metal bowl inside.

I set my door so that it won't lock behind me. The hallway is quiet and still. There are little lamps all the way down to the elevator bank—they have swirly white glass covers that make shadows on the beige walls. On Agnes's door, a bunch of curly ribbons and streamers frame a metallic firework decoration. She must have done that tonight, because I didn't notice it earlier, and it's not something I'd miss. The only other color out here is the dark-blue carpet, which is surprisingly soft to sit on, I realize, as I settle in on the other side of the bag.

"What's in there?" I ask.

"Party things." Agnes tugs at a loose thread on one of her slippers. She's in her pajamas, I realize—a button-up top and matching set of pants printed with yellow ducks.

She sees me looking.

"Ducks," she says, pointing to her shirt and laughing. "Quack, quack!" She starts making a duck noise, and it makes me giggle, but I clap my hand over her mouth because I'm afraid someone will hear us out in the hallway.

Agnes pulls away quickly and her face gets stone serious. "Don't touch," she says loudly.

"Oh," I say, leaning away from her. "Sorry."

She takes a deep breath. The very deep kind where you count as you breathe out—she goes down from five. Then she says, "It's okay, Mattie. I just prefer not to be touched."

She sounds like a robot, like someone programmed her to say that, and I feel a cold flash in my chest.

But a second later, Agnes is smiling again. "Mr. Perl told me that in his class I have a special force field that's just for me so no one touches me."

Agnes and I have the same teacher—Mr. Perl. I was really glad when we figured out that I was going to be in her class. But I don't know what she's talking about right now, so I just say, "Oh."

And then she looks at my face, but not my eyes, more like at my nose, and she says, "Whatever happens at school, it's okay."

"What?" I ask.

She doesn't answer, she just looks at her watch. Then she points to the paper hat in my hand and says, "Put that on. It's almost time."

I set it on my head, and she reaches into the bag between us. First she gets out a bottle of water and two plastic cups. She pours some into each one, and it fizzes.

"What is it?" I ask her.

"Sparkly water," she says. "My mom drinks it."

I take a sip, and the bubbles tickle my nose. It feels special.

Then Agnes pulls out two sticks and hands me one. She places the metal bowl between us.

Sitting cross-legged and facing me with the bowl in

the middle, she holds up a lighter.

"What are you doing?" I whisper as she strikes it expertly.

"Making fireworks," she says, and in a flash, her stick is lit and sizzling with bright-pink sparks that fall gently into the bowl.

I smile and touch my stick to hers. It blazes green, fizzing and fiery.

"Make a wish," says Agnes, closing her eyes.

I shut mine tight too. *I wish for lots of new friends at school.*

Then I hear Agnes whisper, "Five, four . . ." and I open my eyes and join her countdown as she stares at her watch, chiming in to whisper-shout, "Three, two, one! Happy New Year!"

We smile at each other through the last flashes of our sparklers, and then we drop them into the metal bowl.

Agnes pulls two tiny plastic bottles out of the bag then, and hands one to me.

Before I can ask, she says, "Go!" and jumps up. She starts blowing into the wand she's taken out of her bottle, filling our hallway with glistening bubbles. When I stand and join in, there are so many bubbles that it's hard to see, and Agnes begins to spin and spin with her arms stretched out to the sides.

Behind the other doors in our hallway, we hear people laughing and singing.

"What's the New Year's song again?" she asks me, falling back to the ground and shaking her head like she's dizzy. I sit down too, and when Agnes and I try to remember what the song is, we crack up and just hum.

"Too many weird words," I say.

Agnes nods. "It's about friends, though."

"Like us," I say, and Agnes's smile gets so big it takes up half her face.

"Mattie," she says, "you're my best friend."

I think about Lily and Josephine. I know they would think Agnes is babyish, with her bubbles and her duck pajamas. But they're not here to tell me that she's crazy or that I'm quiet, are they? And with Agnes, my life isn't quiet at all, on the inside or the outside.

"You're my best friend here too," I tell her. Because the

way I said it, it's not a lie.

"Jay! Christopher!"

Maeve is standing in the doorway, calling my dad's and my uncle's names.

But then I stand up.

"Honeypie?"

She's frowning.

"We were just ringing in the new year, Maeve!" says Agnes, making her voice like a car commercial. "Don't blame Mattie—it was my idea."

Maeve shakes her head like she's trying to clear it.

"Well, get back inside before your mama wakes up," Maeve tells Agnes. "And take all this stuff with you." She moves her finger around in a circle that points to the hats and the bowl and the charred sticks.

We say good night and I go inside with Maeve.

"Are you mad?" I ask, handing over the bubble wand.

"No," she says. Then she laughs. "For a second I thought . . . oh, never mind. I told you you could stay up. I just wish you'd let me know you were out there."

"I'm sorry." I drop my head down and walk into my

room. I really am sorry. I hate disappointing Maeve.

"Honeypie?" Maeve's voice comes softly from the doorway.

"What?"

I look up, and she blows a string of bubbles at me. "Happy New Year."

Chapter 7

On New Year's Day, Mama doesn't get up until I've been awake for an hour already. When she walks out into the living room, her face looks puffy and her eyes are still half-closed.

"I made oatmeal in the microwave," I tell her. She smiles and shuffles into the kitchen. The oatmeal is probably a sticky mess of goo by now, but Mama doesn't say that as she sits down to eat it. She just says, "Thanks, Mattie."

Then she tells me she thinks we've unpacked enough and as soon as she showers and gets dressed we can go to Home Depot to buy paint and stuff for my room—they're having a sale. That's how I know Maeve didn't tell her about finding me in the hallway last night—it's our secret.

Mama gets in the shower, and I turn on the TV. Daddy pads out in his slippers and makes coffee. When he passes me on the way back to his room with a mug, he ruffles my hair. That's when I ask, "Did you have fun last night?" And I find myself hoping really hard that they did.

Daddy stops and turns to me on the couch.

"Yes," he says. Then he stops, but I can tell there's something else. I'm good at figuring out when silences are real and when they're pauses about to be filled. "You know your mama's a little sensitive these days, so be extra kind to her, okay?"

"What's she sensitive about?" I ask.

Daddy rubs his hand over his face like he's too tired to think. "She has to find her way in a new place, look for a job . . . deal with me." He smiles then and adds, "Your mom's never lived anywhere outside of North Carolina, you know."

I nod, thinking that leaving the only hometown you've ever known must be really hard if you've lived there for a whole adult life. I only got to eleven, and it feels weird not to be there.

"Okay, I get it," I say, and before I can invite him to come with us to Home Depot, he's back in his room closing the door and Mama's dressed and ready to go. We don't even have to talk about whether Agnes is coming— she pops her head out her door as soon as she hears ours open, and I'm glad for the company.

But when we get to the store and Mama goes off "to find paper towels in bulk," Agnes starts acting weird. She walks funny because she says she can't let her feet touch any of the lines on the floor of the store. And there are a lot of lines.

"Can you stop?" I ask her, but she doesn't answer and she doesn't stop, and that puts me in a grumpy mood.

When we get to the paint section, she starts reading out the names of the paints in a really high-pitched voice:

"Violet Indulgence!

"Summer's Secret!

"Wonderstruck!"

"That one," I say, needing her to be quiet.

"Wonderstruck looks good." It's a golden yellow, close to the orange that I found on my walls, but different enough to be my own. Also, I like that name.

"Okay," Agnes says, handing me the paper with the paint sample on it.

Then she starts again:

"Rustic Pheasant!

"Maestro!

"Lime Bloss—"

"I already picked one," I interrupt.

She stills, mouth open midshout, and says quietly, "But you need more than one color for your walls."

"*You* need more than one color," I tell her. "I don't. I'm going to paint my walls all the same like a regular person."

I thought I was going to be adventurous, but now that I'm here and Agnes is acting so strange, I just want my walls to look normal. I see a lady near the counter watching us and my face gets warm.

"Why would you paint like a regular person?" asks Agnes.

"Because." I march up to the paint-mixing guy and ask for my color.

When I glance back I see Agnes coming toward me, walking all herky-jerky to avoid the lines again. And there's someone behind her.

A sandy-haired boy is imitating her walk a few feet away. He stops abruptly when I turn, but he and his friend laugh to themselves. Agnes doesn't seem to notice.

I'm suddenly extra glad that I haven't started school yet, because what if someone saw me here, shopping with a crazy person?

Mama comes to find us, and I give her a look that says *Agnes is being a nut!* But I'm not sure it translates because she just smiles back at me, and her eyes are still as cloudy as they were this morning. We go to the kids' bedroom section and pick out some bird- and flower-shaped decals that you can stick onto walls and peel off when you're tired of them. They look like shadows, so I decide they're sophisticated.

On the car ride home, Agnes tells me that she has some leftover blue paint from her room that we can use to make swirls over the gold color I picked out, but I don't say anything back to her.

In my bedroom, the first thing Agnes does is rush to

the windowsill and say, "Let's put these somewhere safe." I take my treasures and place them on the very top of my sock drawer. With Mama's help, we push my dresser to the center of the room, along with my bed and my desk, so we can cover them all with plastic while we paint.

Mama tells us to start in the middles of the walls— she'll work on the edges after she puts tape over the parts we shouldn't paint. Daddy is still in bed, but Mama says we can listen to music if we keep it low. We put on the radio, and Agnes and I sing along to a Taylor Swift song.

I want to ask Agnes why she was so weird at the store, when she's being normal again now, but I don't. We work quietly together, and it feels like we're in our own little world, making the walls around us a glowy gold that will be warm and cozy when we're done. Part of me wishes I could keep Agnes here, in between these yellow walls, where she's my new friend who is never bored or boring.

But another part of me is thinking about two days from now—when school starts. And I feel a heavy blob in my stomach, the kind that sits there when I hear Mama and Daddy argue, or when I know I'm going to have to take a test the next day.

★ ★ ★

That night, I use Mama's phone to call Lily. We talk about how she got a spa gift certificate for Christmas so she and Josephine went to get manicures for the first day back at school. And then she drops the bomb:

"Ryan kissed me!"

"He did? When? What was it like?" My rush of questions sounds excited, but inside I feel myself getting upset as she gives me details. (Soft, kind of wet, but nice. They were out in her driveway with snow flurries all around, which made it extra magical.) Then she says it happened last week.

"Why didn't you tell me sooner?"

"I would've texted you, but you don't have your own phone," she says. "It's weird to have to call your mom's number, Mattie. Sorry, but it is."

I feel like I might cry, but I swallow it down and make my voice sunny. "I start school this week," I say.

"OMG, good luck! I'd be so nervous."

"I am," I tell her. And then I realize that I could use Lily's advice. "Actually, I've started becoming friends with my neighbor."

"Oh, that's great!"

"Yeah," I say. "But she's a little weird."

"Weird like how?"

I tell Lily about the yelling in Home Depot and the crazy walk and the way Agnes acted like a robot when I touched her.

"Whoa—that girl has problems," says Lily.

I sit up straight. "But she's also really fun," I say. "Her room is all different colors and she likes to play this game called Detective where we pretend to be solving a mystery in our building."

"Is she our age?" asks Lily.

"Yeah, she's eleven," I say.

"Oh."

"Why?"

"She just sounds kind of younger."

I don't say anything. I just look down at my feet.

"Mattie, I don't think you should go into school being friends with this girl," says Lily.

"Lily!"

"I'm not trying to be mean, but you don't know anyone else and you don't want to have to walk in and have everyone think you're like her. You're not. She sounds really weird."

I realize Lily is voicing out loud the things I've been thinking in my head, but that makes me feel guilty. Agnes has been nice to me. Am I just supposed to ditch her?

Chapter 8

The first day of my new school life is a Wednesday, and I'm glad I don't have to face a whole week. I look at my clothes for half an hour and end up in dark jeans and a white sweater with a cable-knit pattern. I slip Josh Jensen's twine ring on my finger and give it a kiss for good luck, which is silly, but no one sees. For color, I add red ballet flats, and then pull on my purple puffy coat and try to avoid Mama as I walk out the door and yell, "Bye!" Daddy's already left for work.

But Mama isn't having that. "Mattie, where do you think you're going with those summer shoes on?"

"They're all-season," I tell her, knowing I've already lost this battle.

She holds up a finger. "Wait right there."

I think about making a break for it. I've got the door open and everything. But then she could call down to the doormen and have them stop me at the exit, which would be embarrassing.

Mama comes back with white socks and my brown leather boots, which are actually pretty nice too. I kick off the flats and redo my footwear.

"I wanted a pop of color," I say, my voice sounding whiny even to me. Mama doesn't cringe or criticize. She just goes back into the hallway and comes out with my bright-red headband.

I smile at her and give her a hug, then I adjust my headband in the entryway mirror. My hair is halfway down my back, and the headband actually highlights that, I decide. Good.

"I know you're nervous, Mattie," says Mama. "A new school is a big change. But you'll do great."

"Thanks," I say, patting her on the arm. I already gave

her a hug, so that's enough of this.

"Want me to walk you to the bus stop?"

"It's right outside the building."

"I know," says Mama. I notice that her hair is growing out, and it's kind of messy—she usually keeps it really short and neat. Daddy always said she has a "classic face" that short hair looks good on, but he hasn't said that in a while, not even on New Year's Eve when she looked so pretty.

"I can go by myself," I tell her.

"Are you going to knock for Agnes?" asks Mama.

I nod yes. I've thought about this a lot, especially since I talked to Lily. I need to knock. I have to.

"Good," says Mama. Then she pauses, but I can tell she wants to say more. "Mattie, you've noticed that Agnes is . . . different."

I nod again, thinking about all the things I told Lily. But I don't have to explain to Mama about the weird-ness—she already knows.

"Well," she says. "It's just . . ." Mama can't seem to finish what she starts saying, and I'm in a rush.

So I say, "I'm gonna meet all kinds of different kids here, right?"

"True," says Mama. "But . . . Agnes might be more different."

I look at the clock behind Mama. Why is she bringing this up now and making me feel all sweaty?

"I'm going to knock for Agnes," I say.

She gives me a smile that looks half-happy and half-sad as I close the door. I stand still for a second—I'm more nervous than ever about whether Agnes will be weird at school. But I don't want to go alone.

I knock on 914.

No answer.

Knock, knock, knock.

I lean my ear against the door, waiting to hear footsteps. But there's no sound.

Bang, bang. I knock harder.

Nothing.

Maybe Agnes already left. The knot in my stomach tightens. Would she go without me?

I spring for the elevator, heading down to the lobby and waving to Doorperson Jessica as I push through the front doors and out into the winter air, which hits my face with a smack! I look to my left, where the bus comes. There are three kids there—two boys in green football jackets and one girl in a tan coat that looks like something an adult would wear, all long with buttons and a pointed collar.

No Agnes.

I glance at the doors to the building. I can't go back in now.

The cold air forms a white frosty stream from my mouth as I take a deep breath and let it out. This sure isn't North Carolina.

Then I smile, because Maeve told me that smiling, even when you don't feel like it, can actually make you happier. And I walk toward the bus stop.

As I get near, the boys start whispering to each other, but I don't think it's about me. They're focused on something around the side of the building, and when I look closer, I can tell that it's part of a bird's nest on the ground near the bushes.

I lean over to see more, and the girl in the tan coat says, "I wouldn't do that if I were you. Birds are flying rats, and they have a ton of diseases."

I look back at her, and her ice-blue eyes make my next step unsteady.

"Are there any babies in there?" I ask.

She just clucks her tongue and turns around, making her long brown ponytail flick at me, so I look to the boys.

"Just one baby," says the taller one, who has pink cheeks and a buzz cut and big front teeth. He points a long, thin arm toward the entrance of Butler Towers. "*She* said not to touch it."

I turn. Through the doors, Agnes is emerging in streaks of color. Her pink scarf trails behind her as she skips toward us in a bright-blue jacket and yellow corduroys. Her sneakers are the same pink as her scarf, and her short hair is improbably filled with tiny barrettes in all shades of the rainbow.

"Mattie!" she shouts. "We're saving a baby bird! I went upstairs to see what I could find out online and to get these." She holds up a pair of binoculars. "We're supposed to watch the nest from afar because her mom and dad will probably come back soon."

When she gets to us, she moves toward the nest past the boys, gesturing for me to follow her. Then she looks down at my hand. "You're wearing your ring!" she says, and I'm glad she noticed.

But then I hear the loud engine of the bus and the squeal of its brakes as the door opens for us.

"The bus . . . ," I say.

"Mattie, this is a *life* we're talking about. A baby bird. We can't leave her alone—we need to wait for her parents."

I look over at the other kids, who are all staring at us.

"You'd better not miss your first day of school," says the blue-eyed girl.

The boys shrug and start up the steps, and I stand there looking back and forth, between rainbow Agnes and the big yellow bus.

"You gettin' on, hon?" asks the old-lady bus driver. She doesn't look at Agnes.

I imagine myself staying here with Agnes, missing the bus on purpose and waiting at Butler Towers to watch a baby bird. I think of Mama and her messy hair and chipped nails and half smile.

"I can't skip," I tell Agnes.

And then I step onto the bus and don't look back.

Chapter 9

My teacher, Mr. Perl, thinks he's funny. But not because of his giant square glasses or his shaved head or even his wide red tie, which are the things I find funny about him.

"Mattie Maeve Markham, meet my minions!"

This is how he introduces me to a classroom full of strangers. The desks are arranged in groups of five—four facing one another in a square and one on the end, hanging off. There's a group that has just four kids at the five desks, so I join them, and guess which desk I get? The sore thumb.

Agnes's empty desk is easy to spot across the room

because it has colored masking tape around its edges in a thick border, and part of me is glad that I don't have the option of sitting near her. Would I sit in her group if I could? Now I don't have to decide.

I look down at the brown carpet as I walk over to my desk—it's hard to take in twenty new faces at once, and I can feel them all staring at me. I put my backpack on the floor because I haven't been assigned a locker yet.

You'd think schools would understand how hard this midyear starting can be on a kid and they'd set you up ahead of time, like with a real locker and a teacher who doesn't shout out your full name like a kook. But oh well.

I'm half wishing I were at home with Agnes, making a new nest for a baby bird out of rainbow string or something, when the girl to my left leans over to me.

"I'm Shari," she says, her long brown braids brushing my desk as she whispers and points. "That's Diego and Finn and Bryce."

Bryce has flaming red hair and pale skin and a laugh like a horse's neigh—I heard it in the hallway when I first walked into school. Even sitting down, I can tell that Diego is sporty looking, like maybe he plays soccer, and his lips stretch wide across his face. Finn is the tall, skinny boy from the bus stop.

"Hi, bird lover," he says, smiling at me, and the way he says it isn't mean or anything. It's kind of nice. It makes me wish I'd sat near him on the bus instead of jumping into the first open seat I saw without looking around at anyone.

"Hey," I say back.

"You guys know each other?" Shari whispers.

"She's at my bus stop," says Finn, and I notice that his brown eyes look like a deer's or something, all soft and open. And his teeth aren't as big as I thought at first.

"Oh." Shari sits back in her seat. "Well, I'm glad you're here—what was your name again?"

"Mattie," I say.

"Right, Mattie. Now there's another girl at the table at least."

"Team Four!" says Mr. Perl. "I trust you can chat with our new friend at lunch. For now, eyes on me."

Everyone turns to face the board, where Mr. Perl is drawing a jagged-edged rectangle.

"This is the state of Pennsylvania," he says. "We're

going to learn everything there is to know about our home this month."

Our home? My home still feels far away. But at least Finn is being nice to me, and so is Shari. Sort of. I think.

I glance at the side of Shari's face and wonder if she's going to be a friend. She has pretty hair and she seems outgoing, so those are two pluses. I remember what Lily said about me being quiet, and I don't want anyone to think that about me this year.

But I also don't want to get in trouble with the teacher, so I look down and open up my notebook to start learning about the great old state of Pennsylvania.

After school, I walk past where the bird's nest was, but I don't see it on the ground. I hurry inside—it's cold here!—and when I get up to my apartment I let the door slam behind me. I smell gingerbread cookies baking.

"Mama!"

She's wearing her favorite blue-striped apron and her hair is pulled back in a headband like mine.

"You look nice," I say.

"I had a job interview!" Her eyes are bright and she

seems more like herself than she has since we got here. "It was at this beautiful downtown bakery—the space is an old bus depot." She stops and looks at me. "Oh, but listen to me going on—how was your first day, baby?"

I sit at the counter and reach for a gingerbread lady from the cooling rack. I bite off one arm and smile at Mama. "It was good," I say. And I mean it. The knot that was in my stomach this morning is gone.

Shari asked me to sit with her friends at lunch, and we talked about the TV shows we like—they're all into the new season of *America Sings!*, which is my favorite. Shari and I even got shushed while we were walking together in the hallway because we were laughing too loudly after she tripped over her shoelace. I've never been shushed by a teacher before. Plus, Finn sat behind me on the bus home and told me a joke about a duck kissing a chicken—it made my face get warm. I've never had a boy pay attention to me before. Lots of things happened that usually only happen to other girls.

Mama leans in on her elbows. "Talk to me," she says.

Knockknockknock.

I stop chewing. "It's Agnes."

Mama smiles and straightens up. "I know. Didn't you just leave her?"

"She wasn't at school." I'm not sure what to tell Mama. I don't want to get Agnes in trouble. And I don't want to talk about Agnes right now. I want to talk about my day and Shari, and I might even mention Finn if Mama keeps being cool.

"Is she all right?" asks Mama.

"Yeah, she just stayed home today."

Mama frowns slightly, but then she smiles at me. "Okay. Want me to tell her it's mother-daughter hour?"

I nod, saying, "Not those words, though," and she goes to the door while I stay out of sight. Agnes keeps trying—I hear her telling Mama that I need to come down with her and see the baby bird immediately. Mama's voice stays sweet while she says to Agnes that I'll talk to her later.

When she clicks the door shut, she lets out a big breath.

Then Mama comes back and unties her apron, sitting next to me and breaking the tail off of a gingerbread cat.

She leans in again. "Tell me everything."

Chapter 10

Agnes couldn't save the nest for the baby bird—it was too broken—but she got a strawberry carton and filled it with a soft washcloth and then some pine needles and leaves for the bird to rest on. She tucked it up in the tree near where the nest was, and the parents did actually come back! Even so, Agnes keeps saying she wants to wait until she sees the baby bird fly. She's got a stakeout position with binoculars, and I think she maybe stays there all day. Doorperson Jessica even brought her a folding chair to sit on. "I'm observing like a scientist," Agnes said, and she showed me a giant chart she's making about the birds' feeding patterns.

This all means that she isn't at school for the whole three-day week. I guess her mom is okay with that. So am I.

I sit with Shari and her friends Emily and Robin again at lunch on Thursday and Friday. Finn tells me he has an uncle in North Carolina who's a Wolfpack fan. They're a rival college basketball team—my family roots for the Tar Heels—but it's fun to have something to joke around about. Plus, I think he likes that I know about sports.

Diego and Bryce are really nice too, and it seems like I might have some friends who are boys, which is something else I haven't had since, like, kindergarten. It makes me feel older, and cool, to have a mix of girl and guy friends. Maybe when you're the new girl it's easier for boys to be friends with you. There's no one here who knows that when I was in first grade I got sick on Halloween and barfed all over my ruby-red Dorothy shoes.

Now I'm eleven. I wear soft sweaters and jeans and boots and my hair is long and maybe even as pretty as Shari's on good hair days. She tells me her parents are from "the islands," which sounds really cool, and she has, like, twenty separate braids that swish and swing. I've watched how she flips her hair over her shoulder, and I'm starting to do it too, but in my own way so it doesn't seem like I'm copying.

The only bad part has been Marisa, the girl with the ice-blue eyes from the bus stop, who kind of turns her head away from me whenever I'm near her. I've noticed that Shari says hi to her in the hallway, but it doesn't seem like they're actual friends, so I can mostly just ignore Marisa. I'm glad too, because she has this dark look on her face that hovers like a rain cloud.

On Friday—after telling us about Andy Warhol, this artist who grew up in Pennsylvania and went on to be a really big deal by painting pictures of cans and famous people—Mr. Perl asks if anyone knows where Agnes has been this week. I don't say anything. But when the rest of the class files out to go to the art room, I stay behind and tell Mr. Perl that Agnes is watching over a baby bird, and that I'm helping. I did sit with her to watch a feeding yesterday after school—it was kind of neat. Agnes said the parents were bringing the baby insect larvae.

Mr. Perl smiles and tells me he'll send Agnes's work home with me.

Later that afternoon, when the bell rings, I pretend to study the calendar on the wall of the classroom so I can wait until everyone leaves before I collect Agnes's papers.

"Let's not let her fall behind," says Mr. Perl as he hands me a big brown envelope. "That Agnes is special."

When I get back to the apartment I hear Mama talking on the phone. I freeze in the entry.

"... can't stay at home every day."

Pause.

"I respect that, and the doormen are certainly responsible people, but I don't know that it's—"

Pause.

"I'm glad she's seeing someone, and I understand that she needs her own time, but Agnes isn't an adult, and I'm concerned that—"

Pause. Agnes's mother is an interrupter.

"Okay, then. Okay. Good-bye."

I peek around the corner. "Hi."

Mama is still looking at her phone like it confused her, but she snaps out of it quickly.

"Oh, honey, I didn't hear you come in."

"Was that Mrs. Davis?"

"Yes," says Mama. But then she puts down the phone and asks if I want a snack, so I know she doesn't want to tell me what they were saying.

Knockknockknock.

I think Agnes can hear when I get home. Mama lets me bring my yogurt squeeze pack with me and when I hand over Agnes's homework, I tell her that my mom talked to her mom about her missing school.

She doesn't even care.

"It's okay, Mattie," she says. "My mom understands. She's very present."

"What does that mean?" I ask.

"It means that when she's working, she's focused there. But at home she's all about me. She has good balance, and she's making sure I do too."

"Does that mean you guys are great at gymnastics or something?" I ask, half joking, but honestly confused.

"No!" Agnes laughs an out-loud crazy sound. "It means I don't have to go to school every day if I don't feel like it. Some days yes, other days no. Balance."

"Oh." She seems confident, but I'm not sure she's

allowed, like, by the law, to not go to school. I didn't know that was a thing a kid could do.

"Besides, I'll go on Monday and I'll tell the story of how we were heroes for a baby bird. Maybe we'll get extra credit. Mr. Perl likes things like that."

Then Agnes tells me she wants to go check on the nest, so we head down in the elevator. I think she's right about Mr. Perl, but I get the knot in my stomach again, because I like how things are at school without Agnes there.

When I look at the baby bird through the binoculars, though, I can see that it's getting better, with feathers coming in and everything. I decide I shouldn't worry. At least not right now.

"I'm going to bring in a report about Billie with an *ie* next week," she says.

"Billie with an *ie*?"

Agnes points toward the bird. "That's her name."

"How do you know?" I ask.

"The same way Grandmother Maeve knows I'm a lightning bug! It just *is*!" Agnes shouts, and she spins around happily.

I sort of understand what she means, so I don't ask her more questions.

When Doorman Will comes out to say Mama called me in for dinner, I ask Agnes if she wants to eat with us.

"My mom left me spaghetti," she says, so I don't ask again.

"I'm gonna go up," I say. She nods but doesn't move. As I'm leaving, I turn back and see Agnes aiming the binoculars at the nest again.

"Billie, you are a beautiful bird," she says very quietly, but I hear her. And when I go inside, I see that Doorman Will is at the window, keeping watch over Agnes.

At dinner that night, it's just me and Mama again. Daddy used to be home to eat with us at least a few times a week, but he's still adjusting at his new job, and also he needs to check in on Maeve, so we have to be supportive. Meaning we can't bug him about missing family dinner.

Mama wants to know more about school, and I have lots of things to say, even though it hasn't been a full week yet—it feels longer, in a good way. We talk about how Shari brings butterscotch candies and shares them with me, and also how Finn is so funny that I almost got in trouble for laughing in class today. I mention Diego too, and how he's very smart and serious, so she won't think I talk about Finn too much.

"That's great, Mattie," says Mama. "What's your favorite part of the day?"

I think. "Hmm . . . at lunch I sit with Shari and Emily and Robin—Emily and Robin have a different teacher, but they're really nice."

"So lunch is the best?" asks Mama, smiling.

"Yeah." I laugh.

Today at lunch, Robin started getting Shari's and Emily's advice about her birthday party planning, and then she turned to me and said, "What do you think, Mattie?" which means I'm definitely invited when it happens. My lunch table is my favorite because there were three of them, but adding me makes four, and Shari and I are in class together all day too, so it seems like we're going to be best friends. It's too early to say those words out loud, but I can already sense it. She asked for my phone number to put in her cell, so I had to tell her how I don't have my own phone. ("It's so lame," I said, and everyone agreed and sympathized with me.) I gave her both my mom's and my dad's numbers, just in case.

I'm feeling happy inside as I sit with Mama tonight and we eat our lasagna, but then she asks me how things are going with Agnes and the happy dims.

"Fine," I say.

She gives me a look that reminds me that *fine* is not an acceptable answer in our family. Daddy says it's a bad word because people use it to stop up a conversation without saying anything.

"Good."

She raises her eyebrows.

"We have fun," I tell Mama.

"I'm glad," she says. "Mrs. Davis says she'll definitely be at school on Monday."

"I know."

"So you'll have another friend to be around," says Mama, and I can feel her looking at my face really hard. So I try to keep it very still.

"Yup," I say.

When we're almost done eating, Mama says, "Well, I'm glad you're liking your new school. And I have news!"

Then she tells me that she's going to start working at a bakery called Blue Sky in downtown Philadelphia tomorrow—the one that was an old bus depot. They just called her this afternoon. "My first shift is tomorrow, so I have to be there at four a.m."

"That's great!" I say. "The cookies worked!"

She nods happily. "They like the blog too."

Mama made batches of fancy cookies and delivered them with her job applications—it was Agnes's idea. She also keeps this baking blog where she tries out recipes and takes really nice photos of what she makes; she has professional lighting and everything.

"Baking is your happy place," I say to her.

"You know I love being home with you too," she says. "I feel a little guilty that you'll have to get ready for school on your own some days."

"I'm old enough," I tell Mama, thinking that I really am. Besides, I don't want her to worry about that—she looks more sparkly right now than she has in weeks, even though she'll have to be up before the sun. She's used to those kinds of morning hours. I think bakers are the earliest risers in the world.

★ ★ ★

That night, I toss and turn for a while, and when I hear Daddy come home I look at my clock: 10:42 p.m. Mama's talking quickly like she does when she's excited, but I can't make out what she's saying except for a few snippets about dessert ideas. I don't hear Daddy respond, but then they put on an old record that they like from when they first met, and even though I don't really like these songs, the muffled sound of them makes me relax and I drift off to sleep.

Chapter 11

On Saturday morning, Mama's gone when I walk into the living room rubbing my eyes, and Daddy tells me we're going to pick up Maeve and go to the Bellevue Stratford for brunch. It's called something else now, but it's a really old historic hotel so Maeve uses the original name. They serve tea with tiny sandwiches and cookies on stacked silver trays. It seems like where a princess would eat, so I used to love it when I was younger and my hero was Cinderella. Now my hero is the spy girl from my favorite book series, but I still secretly want to be a princess too.

It's snowy outside, which would have meant we'd stay

home in North Carolina, but Daddy says they know how to plow the roads here, so we get in the car to go anyway, and he tells me that I shouldn't count on school ever being canceled, like he knew just what I was thinking. Then he says, "Mattie, how *is* school, anyway?"

It makes me feel like I'm talking to some relative I don't ever see, because that's the kind of big question they always ask. Daddy has been like that kind of relative since we've moved. He's never home. I haven't been to his work. We used to go to his office every Wednesday night in North Carolina—we'd make a picnic on his floor right under his painting of a windmill because that was the night he usually had to stay late. No one has mentioned office picnics up here.

I think back to what Mama has said. "It's only been a few weeks. Daddy needs to settle in. We need to be supportive."

"School's good," I tell him. "I like my teacher." I really do—Mr. Perl isn't as goofy as I thought on the first day. He has a fun way of teaching us things, like after our morning lesson we play a quiz game later in the day where he asks questions about what we learned and we have to buzz in as teams by dinging a bell and answering. We're building up points that are tracked on a board in the back of the room; whichever team wins gets to pick the location and the theme of the end-of-school party for our class.

"That's great," says Daddy. "And you've met some friends? I mean, besides Agnes."

I don't really like the way he says "besides Agnes." It seems like he's not counting her, and I wonder if Mama's told Daddy about the weird things Agnes does sometimes.

"Yeah," I say. "At lunch I sit with Shari and Emily and Robin."

"Great," says Daddy. "It's good to have lots of different friends."

I look at his face closely. He's smiling, but he doesn't really seem happy. Then the car gets quiet, so I ask, "Is Maeve okay?"

"She's fine," he says. When we pull up to a red light, he turns and looks at me. "You know that Maeve's getting older and some things may change, but you don't have to worry about losing your grandmother."

I nod. "I know." But my body stiffens—that thought had never crossed my mind until he said it.

★ ★ ★

My grandmother's hands don't stop moving when we sit down at the Bellevue Stratford. We have a corner table with a floral tablecloth covered in see-through lace. Maeve has on white gloves that go up to her elbows, and she brought a pair for me too. Mine are short and pink with bows at the wrists.

"We must wave our arms about as we lunch, so we can show off our gloves," she whispers to me. Sometimes she thinks I'm still six years old, but I don't mind. I feel like we're at a costume party. The waiter is in on it too—he's in a tuxedo, and he bows after I order my tea.

We get a tower of muffins and sandwiches and cookies and cream and jam.

Then Maeve asks me to tell her more about "that lightning bug of a neighbor."

"We rescued a bird named Billie with an *ie*," I tell her.

Maeve's eyes widen and sparkle. "Billie with an *ie*!" she says, clasping her gloved hands together. "Brilliant. What's she like?"

"She's a baby," I tell her. "Agnes is going to do a report about her for school."

"Has Agnes been *going* to school?" asks Daddy. I didn't even know he was listening because he hasn't looked up from his phone. Even now he's scrolling with his thumb.

"She's been out a few days," I say. "But I think it'll be okay—Mr. Perl likes Agnes."

"And why wouldn't he?" asks Maeve. "Christopher, put that contraption down and have tea with your family!"

Maeve doesn't raise her voice, she just makes it stronger somehow, and that means everybody listens. Daddy puts away his phone and reaches for a sandwich. It's a tiny triangle, and it looks silly in his big hand. He swallows it with one bite and wipes his face on a cloth napkin.

"Mattie, I thought you and I could work on painting your room today," says Daddy.

I look at his face to see if he's joking, but I don't think he is.

"Mama and Agnes and I painted it already," I tell him. "Right after New Year's Eve."

I see him freeze for a minute, like I've hit pause on a TV show, but then he flashes a smile. "We'll put up some posters, then," he says. "Maybe make use of those stars you got in your stocking."

"That would be great, Daddy." I've actually been waiting for him to help me with those—I want them on the ceiling, but it's hard to reach, even if I stand on the bed. Or even on a stack of pillows on the bed, which Agnes told me to try. Turns out that's not easy to balance on.

"Oh, you can create a whole world with those stars," says Maeve.

"I know," I say. "Agnes has a book about stars that shows you what the signs look like—Virgo and Taurus and all that. She's going to help me make the ceiling look like the real sky."

"That girl," says Maeve, with the good kind of sigh in her voice. "You picked a fine friend, Elodie."

"I'm Mattie," I say, laughing. But my grandmother looks confused for a second.

"Who's Elodie?" she asks.

Daddy puts his hand over hers. "Elodie is Jay's daughter, your other granddaughter," he says. "This is Mattie, my daughter."

I frown. Why is Daddy talking to Maeve like she's a

little kid? She just mixed up my name for a second.

I smile at my grandmother, and she smiles back. "Mattie," she says, and I nod to reassure her. Then we pick up our cups and clink them together with our pinkies in the air.

Chapter 12

Two minutes after Daddy and I get home, I hear a *knockknockknock* at the door.

"It's Agnes," I tell him, and I watch for his reaction.

"Well, ask her to bring her star book," he says with a shrug.

Daddy's in a good mood now. He hasn't looked at his phone since Maeve called it a *contraption*. Well, maybe he did in private, but not in front of me, anyway.

When I open the door, Agnes smiles big.

"Billie flew!" she says, opening her arms up in a big circle and flapping them wildly.

"What? Really?" I ask, grabbing my coat. "Be right back, Daddy!"

We race to the elevator and head to the tree, where the strawberry carton is now empty.

"She got more and more feathers and I spent the morning down here watching and finally she just hopped off the side and flapped and flapped!" Agnes is doing the waving-flying thing again with her arms, and she looks like a rainbow spinning top in her colorful scarf.

"That's so amazing," I say. And it is. Agnes *saved* this bird.

"I can't wait to tell our class about it," she says.

I take a deep breath and hope everyone will think it's as cool as I do. They will . . . right?

We head back inside.

"My mom's working, and I have to be quiet," says Agnes. "What can we do?"

"Can we get your star book so we can map out my ceiling?" I ask.

"Sure!" says Agnes. We enter her apartment, and I see her mom frowning at a glowing laptop on the dining room table.

"Hi, Mrs. Davis," I say hesitantly, pausing as Agnes rushes into her room because I've been taught to always greet grown-ups.

She looks up, still frowning, but her mouth quickly breaks into a warm grin. "Mattie!" She closes the laptop. "I'm so glad to see you. Agnes has been telling me about your adventures with Billie and how you've nursed her back to health."

"It's mostly Agnes," I say, because that's true.

"You're a good friend," says Mrs. Davis, and something in her eyes makes me shift my weight. I am dying to disappear into Agnes's room, but I'm stuck. "I've seen a change in my daughter since you and your family moved in," she continues. "Agnes is more herself, more relaxed. Having you around seems like it's done more for her than even her therapist can."

I'm silent. I don't know what to say. I thought therapy was for grown-ups who had, like, really hard things happen to them. Also, does Agnes want me to know about that?

"That's good," I say finally, looking around the room and avoiding Mrs. Davis's intense eyes. If they're this strong with glasses covering them, I'm glad she doesn't wear contacts.

Suddenly Agnes rushes out of her room. "Got it!" she says. "Let's go, Mattie." She pulls me away and through the door and we both yell "Bye!" to her mother and get a "Have fun, girls" in response.

Daddy and Agnes and I sit down on my bed with her book and my package of glow-in-the-dark stickers. I try to forget what Mrs. Davis said to me because I don't want to be as important as therapy. I'm only in sixth grade.

"We don't have enough to do the whole sky," Daddy tells us.

Agnes says, "Of course not! There are more stars in the sky than grains of sand on all the beaches on the planet."

I think that's amazing, and Daddy nods at her. "That's right, Agnes," he says. Then he looks at me. "Well, pick the constellations you want most."

"I'm a Gemini, so definitely that," I say.

"I'm a Libra!" Agnes shouts.

"Leo." Daddy raises his hand. "Your mama's a Scorpio."

"And Grandmother Maeve?" asks Agnes.

"Gemini, like Mattie," Daddy says.

"Let's start with those four," says Agnes, turning to the Gemini page of her book.

The funny thing about these constellations is that they look nothing like what they're supposed to be. The Gemini twins are just two sort-of rectangles. The Leo is hardly a lion—more like a jumble of half circles. But I want my sky to look real, so when Daddy holds me up to reach the ceiling and dot it with a pencil, Agnes stands right beneath us and directs my marks.

"Over to the left two centimeters. No, that's two-point-three centimeters, more right. No, up just half a centimeter. That's down! The other up. There!"

We do this maybe thirty times. I still have no idea how much a centimeter really is, but Agnes keeps talking that way, and it seems to amuse Daddy—he's smiling. His arms must be tired from picking me up and putting me down, but he doesn't say that.

When we're done, Agnes and I lie back on the bed. "I can't tell which one's which," I whisper.

"That's how the real sky is," Agnes says.

I scrunch up my eyes and try to find her stars. "Where's

the Libra again?" I ask.

"There," she says, sitting up. Her fingers trace a path quickly, and I can tell that she really does see it up there in the jumble of stickers.

"Wait till they're glowing at night, Mattie," says Daddy. "Agnes, you did a great job!"

He puts his hand on her shoulder for a squeeze, and I jump up quickly when she flinches so much it shakes the bed.

Daddy pulls away and looks at Agnes, but she smiles as soon as he removes his hand. Then she says, "Thank you, Mr. Markham."

There's a long minute of silence, and I wait for Agnes to explain. "She doesn't like to be touched," I say finally.

"Ah . . . okay," says Daddy. "I'm gonna get some coffee." Then he turns and walks out of the room.

My heart hurts for a minute. Why didn't Daddy just *know* about Agnes, like Mama did? I don't know who to be mad at, so I just feel bad.

But when I look back at Agnes, it's like nothing happened. Like she didn't just pierce our fun, starry day by acting nuts.

"Why are you so weird sometimes?" I ask her. I say it gently, because I'm honestly wondering.

Her face is blank, like she doesn't understand the words that came out of my mouth.

But then she says, "I'm just me, Mattie. And *me* is okay!"

It sounds like something a parent—or maybe a therapist—tells you over and over until you repeat it in your own head, and then out loud. It's like the real Agnes isn't in there for a second.

Agnes's mom knocks later, and when she comes in, she and Daddy talk quietly in the kitchen. But it's right next to the living room, where Agnes and I are watching videos of the night sky on YouTube, so I'm not sure why they think we can't hear. Agnes keeps talking about the telescope she wants, but I'm concentrating on her mom's voice. Mrs. Davis is saying that Agnes has a "social disorder" and "anxiety" that has gotten worse since they left Boston. Daddy asks when Agnes's father is moving here, and Mrs. Davis says, "He isn't." That makes me sit up in my seat, but when I look over at Agnes to see if she heard, she starts talking louder. Then I can't make out what her mom is saying.

I wonder what a social disorder is, and what exactly *anxiety* means, but if I ask with those words, Daddy will know I was eavesdropping.

Then Mrs. Davis comes into the living room and says, "Come along home, Agnes." Just before he shuts the door behind them, my dad tells them that Agnes is welcome here anytime.

Sunday is nice because Mama and Daddy are both at home for once, and we "snuggle down" to watch a movie with hot cocoa and popcorn since it's snowy outside. Daddy even makes Mama laugh twice.

But then Daddy gets a call from the office, and I wish he didn't have to go. He leaves in a hurry after saying to Mama, "Thanks for understanding," and she comes back to the living room with a smile on her face. I think since she has a job now too, she's less upset when Daddy has to work.

She starts making dinner, and the pots bang together with happy clinks, and I ask her to play a game after we eat.

While we lay out cards for Double Solitaire, I say, "*Anxiety* means, like, when you worry about stuff, right?"

"That's right," says Mama, and I hear her being careful with her voice. "But there's nothing for you to worry about, Mattie. We'll be fine now that I've got a job at the bakery, and what's happening with your grandmother is natural and . . ."

She stops talking because she sees that I'm staring at her with my mouth open. I was going to ask about whether people get therapy for anxiety, like even kids, but suddenly I'm not thinking about Agnes anymore.

"I'm sorry, honey," Mama says. "I'm rambling." She runs a hand through her hair. "I just don't want you to think anything's wrong. Everything will be all right."

I hold back from telling her that she just put a lot more *wrong* in my head. "Okay," I say.

"Where did that question come from, anyway?" she asks.

"Nowhere." I nod and slap the table to signal we can start the game. We put aces in the middle and shuffle through our extra cards. While I line up my piles, I'm thinking about how small our apartment is. It seemed fancy at first, with the elevator and the doorman, but maybe we live here because we don't have enough money to have a house in Pennsylvania. And what exactly is "happening" with Maeve? As we slam down our cards as fast as we can, I'm slower than usual, but Mama doesn't seem to notice.

Chapter 13

On Monday morning, Agnes and I go down to the bus stop together. I notice that her door has a copy of the "I Have a Dream" speech and a picture of Martin Luther King Jr. on it. Doorman Will gives her a thumbs-up on the way out. "Knock 'em dead, A!" he tells her. Then he winks at me.

But as soon as we go through the glass doors, I lean to my left a little bit so it looks like maybe we just happen to be walking out of the building at the same time by coincidence. She's carrying a big piece of rolled-up poster board with feathers sticking out of the top of it—her report about Billie.

Walking to the bus stop, I quicken my pace when I see blue-eyed Marisa in her tan-colored coat narrow her gaze at Agnes's project.

I stand on the edge of the curb, and that's when Finn comes up beside me.

"Sit with me on the bus," he says. "I have something to show you."

"Okay." I feel my insides warm even though it's freezing. I don't look at Agnes to see if she overheard.

Josh Jensen's twine ring is scratchy on my finger under my glove.

"Mattie!" Agnes's voice is louder than it should be. I'm three feet away. Why does she shout like that? "I'm going to collect some pieces of Billie's nest for my report. There are still a few here!"

I look behind me and see her poking at the place where she found Billie. With her free hand, she picks up a clump of leaves.

"Ew, sick!" Marisa shrieks.

Agnes stares at the pieces of nest in her hand. Then she looks at me. "Billie's parents made it."

"Are those feathers on your poster from that nasty bird? You're gross, *Rag*-nes," says Marisa, and I hear someone else muffle a laugh.

I point my eyes firmly at the ground. My shoulders tense up.

I stay that way for a minute, until the bus comes. I don't look at Agnes again, and I half expect her to start flapping imaginary wings like she did after she saw Billie fly, but she's silent.

Finn gets on the bus ahead of me and finds an open seat. I approach him slowly. . . . He smiles up at me. He still wants me to sit with him. I do, and then I notice that Agnes is already in the very front seat behind the bus driver with the box in her lap.

My shoulders relax as I count that we're six rows apart.

Finn opens the small front pocket of his backpack and says, "This is what I wanted to show you."

He takes out a pencil box with soccer balls on it, which makes me smile a lot. I'm into school supplies like highlighters and erasers and notebooks—and any boy with a pencil box instead of just a crummy backpack filled with loosey-goosey pens is cool.

Inside he has a red pencil with NC State Wolfpack logos all over it.

"Oh, that's a nice color," I say. "Too bad it has that silly wolf on it."

"My uncle told me Tar Heels were all stuck-up," says Finn, his smile growing. "But I still asked him to send one for you too."

He holds up a Carolina blue pencil with my team's Ram mascot on it, and my brain does a backflip, or three: *Finn talked to his uncle about me. Finn had his uncle send a present for me, which is sort of from his uncle but is really from him. Finn just gave me a gift that reminds me of home, and it means he's been listening to me and he knows me.*

I take the pencil.

"Thank you," I say, and it comes out all whispery, so then I make a big show of taking out *my* pencil box (white with yellow stars) and putting it inside very slowly and carefully. That way I don't have to look at Finn again or say anything for a minute. It feels like my face is glowing, and that might be weird.

For the rest of the bus ride, Finn doesn't speak, but I

feel buzzy inside. When we get to school I glance up and see the back of Agnes's head as she gets off the bus, I tell myself not to worry. I remember what she said to me on New Year's Eve, out in the hallway: "Whatever happens at school, it's okay."

I hope she meant it.

Chapter 14

I watch Mr. Perl welcome Agnes from across the room. He gives her a high five that doesn't touch her hand and then peeks into her rolled poster board.

"Wonderful," he says. "We'll give you some time to talk about this next week and then find a place of honor for your poster—real science!"

Agnes beams and settles into her seat. She's on Team One, which is three desk groupings away from my team. I notice that when she sits down, she touches her toes on the floor but points her heels up. Agnes carefully places one pencil and one eraser on the very corner of her desk. I keep my eyes on her, but she doesn't look my way at all, and my hands start to get clammy.

The morning goes pretty normally. We're learning about the agriculture of Pennsylvania, and I take lots of notes so I can do well in trivia later this afternoon. My team has moved into first place in the points competition.

At lunch I sit with Shari and Emily and Robin, and I guess Agnes stays with Mr. Perl to show him her project or something because when everyone gets back into the classroom, she's at her desk already, reading a book. We haven't made eye contact all day, and I wonder if it's because I'm not looking at her or because she's not looking at me.

"Trivia time!" says Mr. Perl. He puts on his funny flat hat, which he calls his "master of ceremonies garb," and passes out the metal bells that you mash with your hand—one for each team.

The room is silent. Mr. Perl knows what he's doing.

"Question one," he says, making his voice rise like a game show host. "What is Pennsylvania's top cash crop today?"

Ding—"Hay!"—Done.

Before I can even turn my head, Agnes has buzzed in,

answered, and settled back into her seat.

"Correct!" says Mr. Perl. "Everyone, in case you haven't noticed, Agnes is back. So bring your A game."

Shari pouts, and Finn whispers to me, "No one else can win with her around."

"She's a freak of nature," says Bryce.

"Team Four!" Mr. Perl's voice booms over the room. "One-point deduction for talking during the game. Do it again and it's a *five*-point deduction."

Everyone goes silent.

"Question two: What city is the chocolate capital of the United—"

Ding—"Hershey!"—Done.

"Correct, Agnes!"

"Question three: Its crack became its most recognizable—"

My hand flashes out like lightning. *Ding*. "The Liberty Bell!" I shout.

"Mattie earns back the point lost by her team for talking!" says Mr. Perl. "Well done."

One of Maeve's Christmas ornaments is the Liberty Bell—it's this huge bell from the 1700s that broke when it was rung—and I've always loved the little felt crack sewn into it.

Shari pats me on the back, and Finn gives me a big grin.

I look toward Agnes, but she's facing the other direction, hand over the buzzer as she waits for the next question.

Mr. Perl asks ten questions today, and Agnes gets all but two of them—the one I answered and another about a groundhog named Phil that Lee on Team Two got. Lee stood up and made buckteeth and tried to make a noise like a groundhog—it was a weird shrieking. Everyone laughed, and he got the question right. Now I know why Team One was in the lead until last week . . . when Agnes was absent.

That afternoon, everyone at my table grumbles about how it isn't fair that Agnes wins all the points for Team One. "It's not just that she knows the answers," says Diego. "It's also that her hands are crazy fast. Who can even touch the buzzer?"

I think about how good she was at Solitaire. She *is* fast.

"She's *special*," says Bryce. I know he means it in the bad way. Then he says, "There's a reason she doesn't have any friends."

And even though I could say something right then—I could say, "I'm her friend"—I don't.

Chapter 15

After Bryce said the thing about Agnes not having friends, I got quieter and quieter. I wasn't my new self at school. I wasn't even my old self. I was upset.

And then as we were packing up to leave, Shari said, "Why do you wear that string on your finger?"

I glanced down at Josh Jensen's bow ring, and I saw it through regular eyes. It looked dumb.

"Oh, I was just bored earlier and tied it on," I said, trying to play it off. Then I pulled on one end quickly and it came untied, falling off my finger like a scrap on the table. I picked it up and shoved it into my backpack.

Shari looked at my face, but I just turned around

because part of me felt like I was going to cry.

"Are you sick or something?" she asked me as we walked out to the bus circle.

"Yeah, I don't feel very good." It wasn't a lie.

"Chicken soup and I'll see you tomorrow!" she said, flipping her long braids behind her shoulder.

When we get off the bus in front of our building, Agnes walks a few steps ahead of me. My insides are churning, and I think that when I get into my apartment I might fall apart. My face feels like I'm going to—it's all tight and wobbly at the same time. This is awful. Agnes and I didn't say hi all day long, and even though that's partly what I wanted, she must be so mad.

But as soon as we walk through the doors of Butler Towers, Agnes turns around smiling.

"Mattie, did you have a good day?" she asks, as if she wasn't a part of it.

"Um . . . yeah," I say.

"Great!" She runs up to Doorman Will and gives him a high five.

"Amazing Agnes!" he shouts.

She grins and dashes in front of me to push the elevator button. "I have an art project I think we should do today, since I don't have Billie to watch—Joanie gave me some amazing supplies that she found thrown away in the art room."

"Joanie?" I ask.

"The night janitor," says Agnes. "She's my friend, and she cleans up after we leave school."

"Oh." Agnes has friends all over. But none of them are our age. "Do you ever talk to any kids at school?" I ask her as we step into the elevator.

I think I see her stiffen, but I can't be sure because her mouth is smiling.

"Mom says they don't get me," she says. "But you do! Hey, where's your ring?"

She's looking down at my bare finger, and I feel a pinch inside. "I untied it."

Agnes's eyes go wide. "But why?!" She looks more upset than I am.

"I don't know," I say, digging it out of my bag. "I still have it. Here."

I show her the small piece of twine, and she opens up

her palm. "I'll fix it," she says as I hand it to her.

When the elevator doors open, she bounds out into our hallway and stands in front of my apartment, like it's already a given that she's coming over.

And I guess it is.

Then things go back to normal between us, which is crazy. Agnes stops by her apartment to get watercolor paints to use with the funny-shaped brushes, rainbow markers, and pastel chalk that Joanie gave her. Agnes puts two jars of water and a layer of scrap paper down on the dining room table before handing me a thick piece of white poster board. "Mixed mediums," she says. "Let's work with all of these and see what we can do."

Then she zeroes in on her own paper and dips right into the watercolors. I've never seen someone so focused on keeping the paints from mixing on the palette—she cleans her brush completely after each swipe—but she swirls the paints together on her paper and it ends up looking really cool and colorful.

"My dad says the sunset holds millions of colors in it," says Agnes quietly.

"Is he an artist?" I ask. Because I think that would explain a lot.

"He's a gentleman philosopher," she says, and I have no idea what she means, but it sounds nice.

"Is he moving here soon?" I'm being nosy, but I'm also kind of playing detective.

"Yes," she says. Then she looks confused for just a moment, but her eyes clear quickly. "I don't know."

I don't ask any more questions because I can feel something around us now, a thickness, like there's too much air in the room. Parent stuff can do this. I think about how Mama and Daddy have been making the air thick a lot since we moved.

Agnes and I don't talk more while we work, but not in a bad way. Things feel okay, and as we make more art, the air evens out again. By the time we're done, I have chalk all over my pants and my sweater sleeves are covered in paint. When Mama sees us, she says, "Smocks next time, girls." I glance over at Agnes and see that she's covered in colors too.

Then we burst into giggles.

★ ★ ★

Before bed, I use Mama's phone to call Lily. She and I have texted a few times, and I keep telling Mama that if I had my own phone I could keep in better touch, but no luck so far. Lily doesn't answer, and I don't want to leave a confusing message about Agnes, so I hang up without saying anything after the beep. Only I think I waited too long to hang up, so now she probably has one of those awkward voice mails where you can almost hear the person take a breath but it only lasts for two seconds so it's even weirder than if they left no message at all.

I toss and turn—it's hard to get to sleep. I just kind of want to figure things out. How can I be Agnes's friend and keep my new friends at school too? I remember Daddy saying that when he has trouble sleeping he reads a book so he can stop thinking about whatever's keeping him awake. Just as I'm about to reach over and turn on my light, I see a star shining outside my window. I move to the glass and there it is: Agnes's signal.

When it flashes off a minute later, I think she's saying good night. She's saying it's okay. And I crawl back into bed and drift into dreams.

Chapter 16

When Daddy says I have a phone call and hands me his cell, I feel relieved that Lily finally called me back—it's been over a week. But when I say, "Hi, Lil," the voice says, "Who's Lil?"

It's Shari!

I get nervous because this is my first new-friend phone call in Pennsylvania. Besides Agnes, I mean. She and I have reached an understanding. At least, I think it's an understanding. We see each other mostly after school. I mean, we "see" each other at school, but we don't talk until afterward. Agnes acts like that's normal, so I'm pretending it is. Because what else can I do? Everyone at school pretty much avoids her, unless they're making fun of her. She eats lunch in Mr. Perl's room, beats everyone at trivia, and has a calm expression on her face whenever I risk looking directly at her.

Agnes seems completely unaware that sometimes she talks at a crazy-loud volume and when she makes animal sounds or flinches at someone coming close to her, that makes people uncomfortable. You just can't act that way in sixth grade. It wouldn't even be okay in fifth.

"Sorry, Lily's a friend from back home," I say to Shari on the phone.

"Oh," says Shari. "Well, I was just wondering if you wanted to come over and hang out today."

Yes. Yes. Yes.

"Sure."

So Daddy drives me over to Shari's house, which is only, like, ten minutes away, and it's pretty and yellow with a big tree in the yard that has a swing under it. It fits her.

Even though it's cold out, I'm thinking we might make a snowman or play on the swing in front because who can waste all this amazing white stuff, but Shari has other plans.

"We're doing a spa day and a photo session," she tells me. "First, face masks, then manicures, then makeup. After that we'll do a fashion shoot with my older sister's clothes—she's on an overnight trip."

"Okay," I say. And we start.

The face mask recipe Shari found involves both peanut butter and eggs, and it's really icky on my skin. When I wash it off, Shari says, "Doesn't your face feel amazing?" And it does, but I don't mention that that might be because it's not covered in peanut butter and eggs anymore.

When we do manicures, I go first and I choose a sparkly polish that has rainbow flecks in it. "I love the colors," I say when she's done painting my nails. Shari doesn't say anything, but then she chooses this dark midnight blue called Velvet Vixen. She tells me that the rainbow polish is from when she was younger, like last year, and my nails suddenly look babyish to me.

Shari's sister's name is Tanice, and everything in her

room is monogrammed, from the red-and-white comforter to the gold curtains to the giant circle mirror on the wall that looks like she signed the bottom in lipstick. It makes me nervous to go in there because Tanice seems really into her stuff. I hesitate in the doorway, but Shari waves me in. "My sister has all the makeup!" she says.

So we sit half and half on the spinning circular chair in front of Tanice's big mirror, and Shari takes out more blush, eye makeup, and lipstick than I've ever seen in one place outside of the drugstore.

"Close your eyes," she says, and I do. She starts with a pencil really close to my lashes, and then she's brushing my lids lightly with the eyeshadow applicator.

"I'm really glad you moved here, Mattie," says Shari, and her breath is soft on my cheek. It smells like the butterscotch candies she's always eating.

"Me too," I say through my teeth, partly because I don't want to move my face too much while she's applying makeup and partly because I have no idea how my breath smells and she's really, really close to me.

I hear Shari click the eyeshadow shut, and I look to see her getting out some blush.

"I was sad at the beginning of the year because Emily and Robin were both in Ms. Stoddard's class," she says, starting in on my cheeks. Ms. Stoddard is the other sixth-grade teacher. "Even though we got to eat lunch together, they were getting to be better friends."

"Mm-hmm," I say. I can see that happening. Robin and Emily do seem close—they have inside jokes from being in class together all day. And I guess Shari and I are starting to have those too. The thought of that makes me feel warm inside.

She pauses and leans back to look at my cheeks. "Hmm . . . I guess you need a different color," says Shari, and then she giggles. I turn to the mirror and realize that Tanice's blush shade is for darker skin—it looks too harsh on me.

"Whoa!" I laugh.

"Let me blend it," says Shari, and she grabs a light-pink powder to mix in.

When she starts to do the soft brushing on my cheeks again, I tell her that I know what she means about Robin and Emily. "My friends Lily and Josephine from home are becoming better friends with each other. I can tell even just by phone calls and stuff."

I silently think that even the phone calls aren't happening anymore.

Shari nods. "Moving must be hard."

"Yeah," I say. "It's kind of sad." I stop but then I keep going, because it's not *only* sad. "But it's also kind of fun," I say. "Meeting new people, I mean."

"Well, I'm glad you're here," Shari says again. "It makes things better." She stops and holds the blush brush in midair. "Also, now your cheeks are better too."

I start to turn, but she puts her hand up and says, "Wait! You need a reveal moment at the end. Let me finish."

Shari opens a mascara tube and tells me to look up before she sweeps the bristles lightly against my lashes. It makes me blink a lot, but it's over quickly.

Then she moves on to my lips. "Open your mouth just a little," she says. I do, and she gets out a gloss wand and paints me with a bright pink.

When Shari puts down the gloss, she claps her hands together. "All done!" I start to open my eyes, but she says, "Wait! Let me spin you." So I close them again, and she stands up and centers me on the stool. Then she takes ahold of my shoulders and makes me rotate one full turn.

I laugh. "Okay, okay, can I look now?"

"Yes."

When I open my eyes and stare into the mirror, I don't recognize myself at first. Long lashes, black-lined eyelids, flushed cheeks, shiny lips. Shari is good at this! My face looks like me, but kind of . . . brighter. Older. Like a teenager.

"Now you do me!" she says, and she closes her eyes and waits.

Chapter 17

This morning, Agnes knocks and she's holding out her hands in two fists when I open the door.

"Pick one!" she says.

I tap her left hand and she opens it up to reveal Josh Jensen's ring, back in bow form like I'd never untied it.

I slip it onto my finger, knowing I won't wear it to school anymore but also so glad it's back to its real shape. "Thank you." I wish I had something more to say. I can tell by Agnes's smile that she knows how much I mean it.

Then she shows me her door. It has the white hearts that we cut out of lacy paper earlier this week. Agnes framed them on pink and red tissue paper so apartment

914 looks like a love explosion. I tell her that and she says, "Oh good! I was going for LOVE!"

Valentine's Day is soon, and I got a card in the mail yesterday from Lily and Josephine—a joint one. I guess it was nice of them to remember to put a real letter in the mail and everything, but the stamp and the envelope and the way they signed it together made me feel even farther away from them.

Agnes says her mom has to work and she wants to come with us to my grandmother's today. When I call to ask Maeve, she gets a singsong in her voice and says, "Of course. Tell that lightning bug I've been waiting for her to visit!"

Mama always works Saturdays at Blue Sky Bakery, so Daddy and I have been going to Maeve's house on the weekends a lot. She's doing a big "packing-up" project with some of her things for a yard sale, and I'm helping her. Maeve has trouble labeling the boxes. I found one marked "kitchen" that was full of summer clothes, and another marked "Felix" that had gardening tools in it. Dad said that Felix had been their cat when he was a kid, but that didn't explain the gardening tools. So it's good that we're there. Also, she stumbled on her front steps over the weekend and she has a badly sprained wrist—I want to sign her cast.

It's unusual to be with Agnes on a Saturday because she and her mom usually spend weekends together since Mrs. Davis works so much during the week. I guess that's part of Mrs. Davis being "present" and "balanced." I also suspect that Agnes has therapy on weekends, but she's never told me about that, so I don't bring it up.

I like being friends with Agnes, as long as we're at home and it's just us. So I'm nervous when Daddy drives us into the city to Maeve's big old row house. But the moment we walk inside, I realize it'll be okay.

It's not because Agnes is polite to Maeve—most kids are like that with grandparents. And it's not because she tells Maeve right away that she likes how the sun hits the blue-gray stones on the walkway outside. It's something about the way she looks at each part of Maeve's house—carefully, like she's memorizing the details—that makes me glad I'm sharing it with her.

"The game is afoot!" says Maeve, after we've taken off our coats and settled into the dining room to have lemonade and ginger cookies. Maeve and Daddy are drinking coffee, and her cast is a new kind—it's made of some type of plastic that we can't sign, which is disappointing. But at least there's a game!

Maeve is always making up detective clues for me to follow. It's one of my favorite things, but last year, when I tried to explain it to Lily and Josephine, saying that maybe we could set up a mystery hunt for each other, they looked at me like I was crazy and then went back to watching their favorite YouTube star, this fourteen-year-old guy who, I'll admit, has dreamy eyelashes and an amazing voice. So I pretended I was joking.

Agnes is sitting straight up, eyes sparkling. Maeve meets her gaze.

"There's a blue marble egg missing from the bowl on the coffee table in the living room," says Maeve, raising one eyebrow. "I'll need your help to find it."

"Yes, sir!" shouts Agnes, her voice very serious.

I laugh into my lemonade as Agnes pushes her chair back from the table. "Let's go!"

When we look at the bowl in the living room, there's a tiny slip of paper underneath the remaining marble eggs.

I read it out loud: "I guard the keys with a silent vow."

Immediately, she shouts, "The monk!"

My mouth drops open. I know where the next clue is, but how does *she* know? In the entryway is a gigantic gold-framed mirror, and underneath it is a wooden monk figure that has a hook on the back to hold Maeve's keys.

When we get to the monk, Agnes finds a folded piece of paper underneath his bent knees.

"Button, button, who's got the button? I do, even though I'm not wearing any clothes," she reads. Then she walks straight into the living room, with its gold carpet and cushy red couch. She heads for the reading chair in the corner, the maroon-colored one with the deep cushion. "Buttons," she says, pointing. And she's right: set into the back of the chair is a pattern of buttons. We hunt around and find clue number three under the back left leg.

The search goes on and on like this—Agnes solving clues in record time while I follow her around like a surprised pet. The only moment where I have the chance to get involved is when clue number eight mentions a painting on the second floor, which Agnes hasn't seen yet.

We find the marble egg tucked into Maeve's sewing chest after twelve clues, in less than thirty minutes. The game usually takes me at least an hour.

How is Agnes so smart? It's like her brain works faster than other people's, or in a different way somehow that makes a really complicated puzzle look like a full picture to her right away.

When we bring the egg back to the dining room, Maeve and Daddy are still having their coffee.

"Well, you must have skipped a few clues, Honeypie," Maeve says to me, wide-eyed.

I shake my head no. "Agnes solved most of them."

"That's not true, Mattie," says Agnes, holding the egg up to the light and studying it carefully. "You were a very helpful assistant."

That makes Daddy and Maeve laugh, and I don't mind. We won the game in no time at all, and Agnes was so into it that Maeve lets her keep the marble egg. Agnes acts like it's a precious jewel.

"Will you girls help me pack up the other eggs?" asks Maeve.

"You're selling them in the yard sale?" My eyes go

wide, because I've been playing with those eggs since I was really little.

"I'm just putting them away, Elodie," she answers slowly. "For safety."

"She's Mattie!" says Agnes in a cheerful voice. Maeve smiles in our direction, but she doesn't look either of us in the eyes and she doesn't correct herself.

My stomach clenches.

"We'll be careful with them," says Agnes, patting Maeve's good hand. "Do you have tissue paper?"

Maeve stands and walks over to open her marble-top table with the stationery drawer, where there's a collection of soft rainbow tissue paper.

"We'll wrap them according to color," says Agnes, picking out sheets of purple, green, silver, and gold to match the eggs.

Daddy goes downstairs to grab a box from the basement for us, and Agnes and I head into the living room, where I hand her the eggs and she wraps each one with slow hands.

When we're done, I tape up the box and use a black magic marker to write "Marble Eggs" across the top. Agnes and I carry it into the dining room together.

"Thank you, my darlings," says Maeve.

I nod, not sure what to say because I feel sad about putting away the eggs and I'm not even sure why.

"Packing special things is hard," says Agnes, and I see a gleam of light in Maeve's eyes. That's what she needed to hear . . . I wish I'd said it.

Later, on the ride home, Agnes tells me that the kitchen is her favorite room at Maeve's. That surprises me, because it's really small and not as grand as the rest of the house. When I ask her why, she says, "Because it has a deep sink and a half-sized oven with two blue-flame burners and a green step stool so Maeve can reach the top cabinets."

And those are the exact reasons why it's my favorite room too.

Chapter 18

This week, Agnes gave her presentation about Billie, and it seemed like it was going okay—she knew so much about how to care for a baby bird and her poster was really cool, with 3D parts and even a painted image of Billie in the corner. But then Lee started making tweeting noises from the back of the room. Mr. Perl silenced him, but after that I felt like I could hear every little twitter, and it was like the whole class was laughing at Agnes in a quiet way.

Finn and Bryce started talking about going to the mall after school on Friday. They kept bringing it up, saying they were going to get new sneakers and also probably see a movie or something.

Now it's Thursday, and when we get off the bus to go home, instead of waving and heading toward his own neighborhood, which is down the hill from Butler Towers, Finn says, "Hey, Mattie—wait," and I stop walking.

I see out of the corner of my eye that Agnes is going inside, and I watch her stay still in the lobby, not looking back, but waiting for me to come in too, so that our out-of-school friendship can resume.

When I turn to Finn, he's standing very close to me. My arms are holding a book to my chest, and his coat sleeve is almost touching mine. I can see the shadows of his eyelashes on his cheeks and a tiny chapped part of his lip as he says, "Do you want to go to the mall with me and Bryce tomorrow?"

"You and Bryce?"

"Yeah, he's asking Shari to go, and I thought I'd . . . you know, ask you."

He looks down and shifts his feet in the snow, stepping back a little.

"Okay," I say.

His head snaps up, and I'm hit with the warmth of

Finn's big-toothed grin. It makes me smile involuntarily back at him.

And we don't say anything for a minute, just smile at each other. Until he says, "Awesome," and I say, "Yeah," and then a squishiness that isn't all bad overtakes me and I turn to go into the building. When I look back at him, he's still standing there grinning at me, and it makes me feel like I am lit by the brightest part of the sun.

Agnes is waiting in the lobby, and she says, "How was your day?" like she does each afternoon.

But I don't feel like cooking or cutting paper hearts with Agnes today. I want to talk to Shari and tell her that Finn asked me to go to the mall and find out if Bryce asked her and what she said, and if the four of us are going to the mall together, what does that mean?

In the elevator, Agnes is telling me about how she wants to paint more pictures of Billie and all I can think about is the curve of Finn's smile. I try to replay each word he said to me, and I want to write it down so I'll always remember.

But there's no avoiding Agnes.

Upstairs in my apartment, she gets out the ingredients for a recipe she wants to make and tells me to prep the carrots, so I start peeling. She's talking, but I'm not listening, and it doesn't seem to matter. She just keeps going. I tune in for a minute, and she's saying something about the shapes of the clouds and how they fit her moods perfectly each day, and I just say to her, "I have to do something."

I walk out of the kitchen, leaving half the carrots unpeeled, and go to the computer in the living room, where I open my email to message Shari.

MMM: did b ask u?

SHARSTAR: y! F and u?

MMM: y!

SHARSTAR: do u like him?

MMM: do u?

SHARSTAR: idk

Suddenly, I feel Agnes's breath on my ear and I turn around to see her leaning over.

"Is that Shari?"

"Yes," I snap at her, closing the laptop.

"What were you typing about?"

"Nothing," I say. I'm mad at Agnes, and I'm not even sure why.

"Okay." She shrugs. "Then let's finish!"

She's smiling her big smile and is not upset or anything at being left out of the conversation with Shari, and I don't get Agnes at all.

But I want her to go home. So I say, "I'm done. Why don't you go to your own apartment now?"

"We're making a recipe," she says matter-of-factly. "We have to finish."

That's when Mama comes in and says, "Agnes, maybe you and I can work on the food and let Mattie have time on her own." I wonder how much she's heard, because she seems to know a lot.

"Okay," says Agnes. She walks back to the kitchen without looking at me.

Mama smiles. "Chat with your friend," she says. "I'll prep."

She starts to walk away, but then I shout-whisper, "Mama!" and I wave her back over to me, so she leans in close.

"Can I go to the mall with Shari and Finn and Bryce tomorrow after school?"

"Of course, baby," she says. "Do you need me to drive you?"

"No, we can take a bus from school that lets us off near there, but can you pick me up after?"

"Sure," she says. Then Mama looks toward the kitchen. "Is Agnes going?"

I shake my head no, and I can tell that Mama understands that not only is Agnes not going but she doesn't know about this.

Mama nods and heads into the kitchen.

Maybe I should worry about how Agnes will feel, but maybe she won't even care. She doesn't seem to mind that we're not friends at school, and this is with school friends, so it's not part of our thing.

Besides, I want to keep hold of the warm, bright feeling that's been buzzing in my skin since Finn smiled at me this afternoon.

So I open up the laptop and find Shari again. I type, *i think I like f.*

Chapter 19

"Those would look so cute on you," I say to Shari when she holds up a pair of dangly gemstone earrings at Leila's Finery, a stand in the middle of the mall that has sparkling jewelry and shiny headbands and silver picture frames.

"You should get your ears pierced," Shari says.

I nod. I know I should. Maybe I will.

"Here." Bryce appears from around the corner and thrusts a smoothie from Juice Jungle into Shari's hands.

"Is it mango?"

"No way, it's blueberry—my favorite."

"Why would you get me *your* favorite smoothie?"

"Blueberry is way better than mango," says Bryce with a cocky grin. "You'll see."

"Bryce Colter!" Shari stomps her foot.

"Hey," he says, smirking at her. "You're lucky I even got you a smoothie. These things are four bucks!"

Shari rolls her eyes and turns her back, but I see her smile when she takes a sip and I can tell she kind of likes Bryce even though he acts like a minijerk sometimes.

"Hey." Finn bumps me gently from behind and hands me my smoothie. I try it. Strawberry banana, just like I wanted.

"Thanks." I smile up at him, and when I meet his eyes his face breaks into a grin too. It's like we're cartoon characters who can't stop smiling at each other.

If I didn't think it'd get stinky, I'd probably save this smoothie cup for my treasure collection.

We sit down on the edge of the fountain in the middle of the mall, and Finn opens up the front pocket of his backpack. "Ugh, not again!" He winces as he pulls out a crazy-looking food item wrapped in foil.

"Is that a . . . cookie?" I ask. It's a bluish-purple lump, but it has sugar crystals on it, so maybe . . .

"Looks more like Play-Doh," says Bryce. "Is your brother baking again?"

"Yup." Finn walks to a nearby trash can and throws away the purple blob. Then he comes back and sits down. "My older brother thinks he's going to be the next . . . uh, famous baker person."

I laugh. "My mom bakes a lot," I say. "Actually, she does it for work."

"That's cool. All my brother does is find recipes on the internet and experiment," says Finn. "Usually, the results are kind of awful, but he tries to make me eat them anyway."

"You've gotta start somewhere," I say. And I realize that's something I've heard Maeve say, and it sounds old-fashioned out loud.

But then Finn says, "I like the way you talk, Mattie." I don't know if he means my accent or what I say, but it doesn't matter. My face tingles with warmth.

We walk around the mall some more, and Finn mostly talks to Bryce and I mostly talk to Shari, but it still feels like Finn and I are there together, and when Mama picks us up at six I don't want any of it to end.

"You girls look happy," Mama says as I get in the backseat with Shari.

"Mama!" I say, but I don't think Shari heard the tease in my mom's voice. She lives near the mall, so we're taking her home, and I'm glad because it seems like another step in our friendship for us to ride in my mom's car together.

Shari is all excitement and laughter, her braids swinging around her shoulders as she rolls her eyes and talks about how conceited Bryce is.

"He thinks he's so smart," she says.

"But you like him, right?" I ask.

"Yeah!" She's smiling big and then covering her face with her hands before she explodes into giggles. It's contagious, and soon I'm laughing too, and Mom is eyeing us in the rearview mirror like we're crazy girls.

We drop off Shari, and I move into the front seat. For the rest of the ride home I grin and look out the window. I don't even want to talk about Finn right now, I just want to think about him in my head.

But when we get back to Butler Towers and the elevator doors open on our floor, I see a solitary figure in the hallway.

Agnes P. Davis.

She's standing straight up, her head centered in one of the lacy paper hearts on her door. It's like she's keeping watch over our entrance, and Mama squeezes my shoulder as we walk toward her.

"Mattie, where were you today? You weren't on the bus and you weren't in the lobby and you weren't anywhere at four twelve p.m."

Mama opens our door and says, "Do you girls want to come inside?"

"No," I say, annoyed. I don't want Agnes to come over. I stay in the hallway and face her as Mama waves at Agnes and then steps in and softly closes the door.

Agnes didn't look at Mama. Her eyes are on me, and she doesn't flinch. "Where were you at four twelve p.m.?" she repeats.

"What is four twelve p.m.?"

"That's when we're home. It's the time the bus drops us off and we walk into the lobby and then we're friends again."

"It doesn't work that way, Agnes," I tell her.

"It *was* working! It was!" she says, and I can't argue

really. So I just say, "You're so weird."

"I'm just me. And *me* is okay!"

"But you act weird all the time," I tell her. "Why do you do that?"

She stares at me. I decide examples might help.

"Like this week when Mr. Perl was talking about Asia and you just raised your hand and then started naming every single country in this robotic voice . . . what was that?"

"I was adding to the lesson," she says.

"You were being crazy," I tell her. "And then you started making loud noises when we talked about indigenous animals."

"Lee does that all the time," she says. "Why is it funny when he does it but not when I do it?"

I pause. She's right. Lee does like to make strange sounds and everyone usually laughs. But it's something about the way Agnes does things. It's just . . . weird. That's the only word I can think of over and over, but I don't know how to explain it to her.

"You make no sense, Agnes," I say.

"I always make sense," she says, and it actually seems

like I've offended her. But then she smiles.

"I'm going inside," I tell her. I cannot handle the weird-ness.

"Great," she says. "My mom got me this new set of invisible ink pens, so we can write mystery notes to each other and—"

"See, that's what I mean," I say. "You think I want you to come over? I don't. I'm going into *my* apartment. You're not coming with me."

Her face is blank.

Then she asks, "Were you at the mall with Finn?" She isn't looking at me; she's looking at the wall behind me. But she knows more than I thought she did—maybe she does pay attention at school.

"Yes," I say.

"And you like him."

"Yes." But it doesn't feel like I'm doing the fun confiding-in-a-friend thing. I'm just trading facts with Agnes. She doesn't want more than that.

"Why?" Her eyes move to my face then. Not my eyes, but more like my left cheek. It annoys me, and I sigh out loud.

"Because!" I shout.

"'Because' isn't a reason for something," she tells me. "You have to have real reasons for things, you know. You're the one who makes no sense."

Her voice is calm and even, and I wonder if she ever reacts normally to anything. Or maybe she's just a low-talking arguer like Daddy, and it makes me want to scream!

"Maybe I don't make sense!" My voice is really loud now, so loud it scares me, but I keep yelling. "Maybe I shouldn't have let it be this way, but you shouldn't have either! Sometimes I wish you weren't here at all!"

I turn away from her so I won't have to know if she feels anything about me closing the door in her face.

Chapter 20

I don't see Agnes all weekend, and she isn't at school on Monday. When Mr. Perl asks me in front of everyone if I know where she is, Shari tilts her head at me funny and Bryce raises his eyebrows. I'm afraid they'll think I'm weird like Agnes just because I hang out with her sometimes.

So I shrug and say, "How would I know where she is?"

And Mr. Perl frowns.

Finn is extra nice to me, and he drops off a Hershey's Kiss at my lunch table, which makes Shari and Robin and Emily go "Oooooh."

When I get home, I close my front door really quietly,

because maybe if Agnes doesn't hear it, she won't come over and act all crazy.

"Hang that up, please," Mama says when I walk into the living room and throw my coat on the couch.

I roll my eyes, but I do it.

"I talked to Mrs. Davis today," says Mama. "She told me that Agnes's dad is coming to visit later this week, and Agnes had an extra therapy session today."

I feel a nervous tingle inside. But outside, I shrug. "Why are you telling me?"

"I thought you might have wondered why she wasn't at school," Mama says, frowning just like Mr. Perl did. But I just say, "Nope," and I go into my room and close the door because I don't want to talk about Agnes.

Then I sit on the bed and let out a big breath that it feels like I've been holding in all day.

On Tuesday, Agnes still isn't at school and that means our team is getting ahead in the trivia competition. We're just a few points behind Team One.

When Shari answers a question about the Civil War right, Bryce gives her a high five and says, "We're unstoppable without the freak around!"

I know he means Agnes, and my chest wobbles inside. I look up at Mr. Perl, but he's busy writing something on the board. He didn't hear. And no one else says anything, but my silence sounds the loudest, at least to me.

Finn comes over to my table at lunch. He doesn't sit down, but he hovers near Emily and me—we're on the edge. He's swaying from side to side at first, but then he stops and says to Robin and Emily, "Did you guys hear our team is totally gonna win the trivia competition this year?"

"That's awesome," says Robin.

"If you win, what will you pick for the party?" asks Emily.

"Last year it was a pizza skating party at Wheelways," Finn says. "But we shouldn't do that this year because I *cannot* roller-skate."

I look up at him, and we share a smile. Then I'm picturing us holding hands and roller-skating badly together, and I have to look down at the table so no one sees me blushing.

"It's all thanks to Mattie and Shari," says Finn, and

I don't correct him. We are the two best responders on Team Four.

"I don't know . . . it doesn't feel like a true win with Agnes out," Shari says.

I lift up my head.

"She's the real competition," she continues. "She's amazing at trivia, so when she's not around it seems like we're cheating or something."

Finn nods. "That's true."

"Agnes is the girl with the short hair who seems kind of . . . off?" asks Emily.

"Yeah," says Shari. "She's new this year. She's weird, but she's crazy smart."

Part of me wants to add that she's also interesting. And fun. And creative.

But I don't say any of that. Because I'm here at this table with new friends and a boy who maybe likes me and what if it all goes away?

On Friday, Mr. Perl asks me to stay after the last bell, and he gives me a folder full of papers.

"Please bring this work home to Miss Agnes, and tell

her that we *all* hope to see her next week," he says. Then he raises his eyebrows so I'll know he's telling me to be nice to her and get her to come back to school. It's not very subtle, but I say okay.

I don't knock on Agnes's door, now decorated with traced drawings of George Washington and Abraham Lincoln for Presidents' Day; I leave the folder on her welcome mat, which is shaped like a rainbow with clouds at either end. She'll find it, and it's not like anyone's going to steal a pile of paper.

Then I go home, into my room, and open up my closet. I'm invited to Robin's birthday party this weekend—it's all we've talked about at lunch lately, and it sounds like she always has amazing birthdays. Last year she had it at her parents' Chinese restaurant and everyone got personalized fortune cookies, which sounds so cool. This year, it's at a bowling alley, and I have to think about what I'm going to wear because it's a boy-girl party and she invited almost the entire sixth grade, so Finn will definitely be there. He sees me every day, but a boy-girl party is a chance to look *pretty*.

I decide on my lavender sweater with pearl buttons on

the sleeves and a pair of gray jeans with my black boots. I think I'll look slightly nicer than usual without being too dressy. Shari approves of this outfit when I text her a photo of it on Mama's phone, and she says it will still look good when I have to trade the boots for bowling shoes. I'm glad I ran it by her because I didn't even think of that.

When I go to bed and turn out my light, I see the glowing stars in perfect constellations above my head, and I feel a twinge in my chest. I've been remembering what Mrs. Davis said about me being more important for Agnes than even her therapist, and it's making me feel extra terrible. So I peek out the window, just in case, hoping Agnes knows that if she really, truly needed me—like for something serious—she could use our signal. But all I see is a dark brick wall.

Chapter 21

On the Saturday of Robin's party, Mama comes home from baking in the late morning—way earlier than usual. I'm in my room reading, still in pajamas. I'm about to go out and ask her what she made today—sometimes she has fun stories about swirly wedding cupcakes or rainbow meringues for birthday parties—but then I hear Daddy's tense voice and I stop just inside my door.

I can only make out every few words, but he's saying something about Mama's job, and I don't hear her reply, and then Daddy's voice gets louder and I hear him very clearly. "Maybe you should get a real job, then."

"What?!" Mama's voice isn't quiet anymore either and

Daddy says, "*Regular*, I meant a regular job—the food industry is so unstable."

I hear Mama's loud sigh. Then her footsteps come toward my door and I sit back onto my bed with my book.

"Hey, Mattie," she says, all smiles.

"Is everything okay?" I ask. Because I want her to know she can't just hide things from me. I'm old enough to know.

She waves her hand dismissively toward the living room. "Oh yeah," she says. "It's fine."

I almost call her out on her nonanswer, but then she does it herself. "Sorry, that's not an answer, right?"

I nod, and she sits down on my bed as I scooch my legs over to make room for her.

"My manager at the bakery said he thinks he may not need me full-time," says Mama. "Business is down, he's saying, and he's going to reduce my hours."

"But you're the best baker ever," I tell her.

"I'm the newest person there, so I'm the first to lose hours when things get slow."

That doesn't seem fair—nothing seems fair anymore. I wonder whether this means we won't have money for things if Mama loses her job. She's been so much happier, and Daddy has too, since she started at Blue Sky. I don't know what to say, so I just pat her hand.

She smiles. "Thanks, my love," she says. "It'll be okay." And then she asks if I want to go makeup shopping.

"Like real makeup?"

"Yeah. I could use a little lift, and I thought maybe you'd like to pick out some lip gloss or mascara for your party," she says, giving me a sly smile. Sometimes Mama just gets it.

"Okay," I say.

At the drugstore, I choose lavender eye shadow and a soft pink gloss. In the end we don't buy mascara because I remember it being hard to take off after I went to Shari's, and Mama says when you wear mascara you have to keep checking it to make sure you don't have raccoon eyes. I don't want to do that—too stressful.

I'm skipping through the lobby and Mama is carrying our bag when we get back to the building. Then the elevator door opens and—*ding*—there's Agnes P. Davis.

"Hi," I say. I realize that I haven't seen her in eight

whole days. She looks different, like maybe her hair is longer.

"Hello." Her voice is pleasant, but it doesn't really sound like her.

"Hi, Agnes!" says Mama, all upbeat. "Your father's here now, right?"

Agnes nods a very small nod and then steps forward off the elevator.

"I hope you all have a wonderful visit," says Mama.

I want to say something too, but I'm not sure what, so I just move aside. Then Mama and I get in and let the doors close between us and Agnes as she walks toward the lobby.

Mama sighs and leans against the wall. The elevator suddenly feels tight and small, and when I go back to my room to get ready for the party, I keep looking at my closed blinds. I tell myself that if I peek out the window and see a star signal from Agnes, I'll go find her and tell her I'm still her friend.

But when I raise the blinds, there's no star signal—it's just plain brick. It's also daytime, so even if she did want to shine a signal it'd be hard for me to see. I shake my head . . . I'm being crazy. Agnes isn't even home—I just saw her leave. Still, I look hard to be sure the star really isn't there, because I can feel something inside, something that's telling me Agnes might need me.

"Mattie? You ready?" It's time to go, and Daddy's in the doorway—he's driving me to the party.

On the way, I try not to think about Agnes. I'm focused on being the new Mattie, who wears makeup and goes to boy-girl parties and maybe even almost has a boy-friend.

Right when I get to the bowling alley—which is completely covered in purple and silver, Robin's signature birthday colors—Finn comes up to me and asks if I want to bowl in his lane. Duh.

Shari has totally restyled her hair. No more braids—it's short now, in a bob that's smooth and straight. I tell her it looks nice and she says it took hours at her mom's hair place but she needed a change. My own ponytail feels plain in comparison, even though Mama let me put waves in the ends with her curling iron.

I've only been bowling like twice before, and the ball keeps going into the gutter, but luckily no one's very good and everyone mostly sits around eating snacks and talking anyway. Which would be fun, except that Marisa wormed herself into our lane and she's being really loud. I wonder why she's even here.

"Finn! Can you help me find a ball that's better for me? I have the smallest fingers!" she calls out at one point. I swear she's batting her eyelashes, which are totally covered in mascara. She's also wearing a dress that ties at the waist, like one my mom has. But it's tight and she's getting boobs, so it makes her look older.

Marisa's leaning in to Finn as he holds out a light-weight bright-pink ball for her. "Perfect! You found just the one," she says. "I love pink!" *Of course.*

Then she looks over at me and Shari. "You guys can use this one too if you want," she says, all fake nice. I have a red-and-black marbled ball that's heavier, and I silently vow to avoid her dumb pink one.

Shari and I go to the bathroom after we finish a full game of bowling and while I put on my new lip gloss in the mirror she asks me if anything's wrong.

"No," I tell her.

"You're all quiet and not smiling."

So much for trying to be the new me.

"Is Marisa bugging you?" she prods.

I turn on the sink and let the water run over my hands. Marisa *is* bugging me, but so is the thought of Agnes and her dad. I'm nervous and I feel bad, even though that has nothing to do with me. And what if we're running out of money and Mama and Daddy are going to start mean-talking to each other again like they did this morning? My mind is stuffed with worry.

"Yeah, Marisa's annoying," I say, grabbing a paper towel to dry off. "But I'm just having one of those days." That's something Mama says sometimes. I follow it with a sigh, which Mama also does, and it feels natural. I like to sigh, I decide.

I hear the door creak open and my heart drops as Marisa walks in, smirking. "Hey, Mattie. Where's your best friend *Agnes?*"

I glare at her, right in the ice-blue eyes.

"What are you even talking about?" says Shari, rolling her eyes at Marisa.

She turns to Shari with a fake-innocent look. "Oh, didn't you know that your new friend Mattie already has a BFF? She lives with Agnes and they raised that baby bird together."

"I do not *live with her*," I say, my voice low.

Shari is quiet, but she's staring at me now.

"We live next door to each other at Butler Towers," I explain.

"Oh," says Shari. "I didn't know that."

And I can't tell if it matters to her, one way or the other.

Marisa turns, her eyes lit up with mean glee. "You guys hang out every day after school, don't you?"

"No," I say.

"I've seen you talking to her," says Marisa.

Shari steps in. "I've never seen you with Agnes," she says. Then she turns to Marisa. "I think I'd know if they were friends."

"Maybe Mattie doesn't want you to find out," says Marisa. "Everyone knows that Agnes is a freak."

I clench my hands into fists when Marisa locks eyes with me.

"I know you're friends with her." Her voice is so cold and accusing, like she's saying, *I know you ran over my dog.*

"She lives in my building!" I shout, taking a step closer to her to shut her up. "I am *not* friends with her!" Then, before my brain can stop my mouth, I hear myself say, "I don't even like her!"

Marisa smiles with tight lips, and it looks like an evil jagged line.

Then she pushes past me and walks back out to the party. She doesn't even use the bathroom—she just came in here to be cruel (and to make me be cruel too, apparently). The door swings open, and I hear people laughing and yelling, "Spare!" but when it closes again I'm there in silence with Shari by the badly lit sinks.

I catch a glimpse of myself in the mirror and I can't meet my own eyes.

But Shari doesn't seem to notice. She just says, "Marisa is so aggro. That's why Robin and Emily and I stopped hanging out with her last year."

"Huh?" I'm confused.

"Robin only invited her because their moms are still friends and Marisa's parents got divorced last year, so . . ."

"I didn't know that," I say.

"I know it's sad, but Marisa got really mean after that," says Shari, looking in the mirror and inspecting her eyebrows. "It's not like her parents breaking up was our fault. It was weird—we'd been close since we were little, but then it was like she had a new starring role in a movie about girls who turn on their friends."

I stay quiet. I don't know what to say because I feel like I'm in that movie right now.

"She's probably also mad at you because of Finn."

"What do you mean?" I ask.

"They kissed last year on a church ski trip," she says. "They never, like, officially went out or anything, but I can tell she still likes him."

My body goes cold.

Shari shrugs. "Anyway, don't let her get to you. I don't know *what* her deal is with trying to make it seem like you're friends with Agnes."

She points to my lip gloss, which is squished a little bit because I'm making another fist, and says, "Can I use some of that?" So I open my palm and hand it to her and she puts it on, and then we go back to our lane, where

Bryce is pressing the button to start a new game.

Marisa is laughing really loudly at something Finn said, and then he looks over at me and I can't even muster a real smile, because my heart feels like it's underneath a rock.

Chapter 22

Shari's mom drops me off at my apartment building, and all I can think about is how I want to crawl under the covers and be quiet and warm and alone for a while.

But when I open my front door, I hear Daddy talking. ". . . getting worse. We should tell Mattie."

"Tell me what?" I ask, peering around the hallway corner to see them both sitting on the couch.

Mama looks at Daddy and then pats the spot next to her. "Sit down, honey," she says, trying to make her voice sound nice.

I move slowly because it's strange that they're sitting here together and it seems like they are about to confront me about something and I think that they're going to tell me that I'm being a bad neighbor and friend to Agnes and I won't be able to explain how it is at school and how the other kids are and why I don't know how to be her friend.

"How was bowling?" asks Mama, like she suddenly remembered where I was all afternoon.

"Fine," I say. And they let me leave it there without pushing more. Which is when I know something is *definitely* wrong.

I steel myself for defending my friends-not-friends thing with Agnes. I can explain how she was the one who was okay with it being that way, until it didn't work anymore. I can tell them I'm confused.

But instead of talking about Agnes, Daddy says, "Mattie, your grandmother is getting older, and we've made the decision to move her into a retirement community."

"What?"

Mama's voice rushes in. "She's okay, don't worry. It's just . . . time."

Maeve. This is about Maeve. My grandmother's gloved hands and sparkling eyes flash in front of me.

"Why?" I ask.

Daddy looks at Mama, and he says, "It's the best thing for her, Mat. She isn't safe living on her own anymore. You may have noticed her memory is a little . . . spotty."

And then I think about Maeve's arm cast, and the way she keeps calling me Elodie, and how she doesn't label boxes right.

I swallow back the lump in my throat. My parents stay quiet—they're good at that, waiting for me to talk. I appreciate it, but I don't know what to say. Finally, I ask, "Is she okay with moving?"

"We're working on that," Daddy says. "It's hard. Maeve wants to stay in her house, but she just can't. With all the stairs and the space she doesn't need . . . it's—"

"It's not practical anymore," interrupts Mama.

"But shouldn't she get to decide?"

"To a point, yes," says Daddy. "And we've been talking to her since we got up here, helping her to transition slowly and—"

"Wait," I say, putting this together. "Have I been help-ing her pack up to *move?*"

Mama nods. "We thought about it as a yard sale at first because that was easier for her to accept, and we *are* having a sale. . . . It'll be such a relief for her to get rid of some old stuff and move into a smaller space where she can—"

"Get rid of *some old stuff*?" I repeat back.

"Well, she has so much . . . ," Mama starts.

"You're making her give up her memories and throw away her treasures!" I shout. "That will make her brain worse! You don't understand her at all."

I flash back to Christmas, how Uncle Jay called it our last one in Maeve's house. They all knew. Everyone's been keeping this from me.

And then I start crying. It just happens. I can't stop it.

"Oh, honey," says Daddy, coming over to put his arm around the back of my chair. I shrink down so that he's not touching me. I don't want him to touch me.

"This isn't about Maeve's things—it's about her quality of life. Mattie, she has to move. That house is too much for someone her age. And with her mind going . . ." He stops talking, and I see Mama's mouth in a thin line, all concerned. And then I look up at Daddy, who's very serious and worried.

I can't *stand* their faces.

So I jump up from my chair and stomp to my room, turning in the doorway. I slam my door and sink down onto the bed. I think of trying to call Lily, but then I realize she never returned that missed call I made a while ago.

Why is everything changing all at the same time?

Chapter 23

The knots of worry in my stomach are getting more jumbled by the hour.

I call Maeve on Sunday, but she says she's "busier than a bee making honey," and we decide I should go over next weekend. I don't want to wait that long, but you can't argue with a grandmother.

When I pass Agnes's door on Monday morning, I see that it's covered in shiny green wrapping paper and there are little shamrocks cut out of cardboard that fall in rows from the top of the doorway.

"Happy St. Patrick's Day," I say to no one. I was home all day yesterday with nothing to do, so I finished reading a new mystery book and experimented with my lavender eye shadow. I guess Agnes was decorating her door for the next holiday.

If she'd asked me, I could've helped. I even have a sparkly green glitter marker, so we could have decorated the shamrocks with it. I could've asked Agnes how her dad's visit is going, and I could've told her about Maeve and how she has to move.

I sigh, which is my new thing. And when I get down to the bus stop, Agnes is already there. She waits right by the corner where the door opens. When the bus arrives, she gets on first and doesn't look at me at all.

I feel mushed up inside, and I can't meet anyone's eyes. If I see someone straight on, they'll know that something's wrong. But if you don't look people in the eyes you don't feel as much.

One person I'm not looking in the eyes is Finn, even though I sit next to him on the bus. I keep my head down and pick at what's left of my sparkly nail polish. Something about knowing that Finn kissed Marisa has made everything seem off with him. I keep picturing him looking into her cold ice eyes and seeing something he likes.

He must know something is wrong because he hardly tries to talk to me either, and he doesn't come by my table at lunch or try to tell me any jokes during class breaks. On Tuesday, Marisa purposely shoves in front of me and sits with him on the bus. He doesn't say anything about saving the seat for me, which makes me feel like I have an arrow stuck in my chest.

Agnes is at school every day this week, but she's not looking at me even more than before, and when we step off the bus now she doesn't wait for me—she just gets in the elevator, and I can tell that she pushes the close door button so that I can't ride up with her. I walk slowly to help her out with that—I wouldn't want to be in an elevator with me either. I look at the clock in the lobby every day, and I see that she was right . . . 4:12 p.m.

It's the week before spring break, and Shari and her family leave on Thursday to go to the Bahamas. She's been all wrapped up in their plans—their hotel complex has something like seven different pools—and I've been fake smiling along with her. I'm not sure if she noticed, but I'm glad she's distracted. I don't want anyone digging into my mood.

I hear Finn say his family is going to North Carolina over break, and I feel him looking at me when he says it, but I don't raise my eyes.

Mr. Perl notices that I'm being quiet in class, and he makes a joke about my team suffering because I'm "off my game." Bryce tells me I need to step it up.

It's like when things are going wrong, people just pile on and make it worse.

When I get home on Friday afternoon, my apartment feels lonely even though it's warm and smells good because Mama is baking sugar cookies. She asks if I'll help decorate them, but all I can think is that if she had time to bake today before I got home, maybe her hours are getting cut even more at Blue Sky.

"I made fairy frosting," she says.

That used to be my favorite thing, when she mixed vanilla frosting with rainbow swirls running through it— we called it *fairy frosting*. But today it makes me think of Agnes and all her colors, and suddenly it's like I can see this cloud of gray all around me. Not even fairy frosting can chase it away.

I shake my head no and go sit on my bed.

Daddy's home in time for dinner, and when I come out of my room, I see him hugging Mama in the living room. They're swaying slightly, almost like slow dancing, and I hear him say, "It's been stressful. I'm sorry."

Mama steps up on her tiptoes and hugs him tighter. "I know," she says softly. "Me too."

I walk backward into my room, close the door quietly, and bang around for a minute so they know I'm coming out. When I open the door loudly and ask, "What are we having for dinner?" they've already parted. Daddy's setting the table, and Mama's bringing out a steaming bowl of pasta.

We sit down and talk about what's happening on *America Sings!*, how Daddy has a new client at work, and how Mama's magic bars sold well today at the bakery, so maybe her manager will notice. I don't ask about why they were hugging and saying sorry, and they don't ask me why

I've been in a mood all week. But somehow, tonight, a part of me that's been fiddling with the knot of worries in my stomach lets go, and when I relax, some of the knots seem less tangled.

Chapter 24

When my grandmother opens the door for Daddy and me on Sunday, I gasp. There are boxes everywhere. The big furniture—the red couch, the chair with the buttons, the dining room table—is still in place, but the smaller things, the sparkling, special things, are gone. Even the red-patterned rug is rolled up in the corner.

I sink down onto the couch, and Daddy heads into the kitchen. "I'll make tea," he says. Maeve comes to sit next to me.

"What's happening?" I ask. And I mean with the packing, but I also mean with everything.

Maeve smiles at me. "A new adventure."

"I can't believe you're leaving this house."

I see her lip quiver—I know I do!—but she just says, "It's time. I'm an old woman."

"You're not!" I say to her. "If you want to stay, you could stay."

"I want to go." She puts her hand over mine.

"I don't believe you," I say, shaking my head. My grandmother is lying to me.

I stand up and climb the stairs before she can stop me, up to the little third-floor bedroom that's been mine and Elodie's forever, and when I get there I slam the door so it echoes throughout the tall, skinny house. The single bed is child-sized, and my feet almost hang off the edge now, but I still love it. I reach for the old silk comforter with black and red checks, and I bunch it up, burying my face into it to catch my tears. I don't hear anyone coming for me, and I'm glad.

After a few minutes, I calm down enough to lie quietly, but I tell myself that I'm not going downstairs. I close my eyes and I must fall asleep, because when I open them again the sunlight patch that was on the wall has moved up to the ceiling and now it's just a sliver of rose gold.

I hear soft knocking on my door.

"Honeypie? I have snacks."

I don't feel as angry anymore, and I'm kind of hungry. So I say, "Come in."

Maeve is holding a silver tray with a grilled cheese sandwich and green apple slices. She places it on the nightstand beside me and sits down on the end of my bed.

There's a part of me that wants to stare at the wall and not speak to my grandmother, but a bigger part just wants to hug her and bury my face in her soft sweater and smell her Shalimar perfume. So that's what I do.

"Shhh, shhh," says Maeve, and even though I'm not crying I like her calming me down this way. We sit like that for a few minutes, and I stare out the double-paned window. I've always liked the way the thick glass makes the blue sky look wobbly, like it's got extra energy pulsing through it. Like maybe that's where fairies and wizards and magic live, in the wavy part of the sky that only looks this way through these windows on the third floor of my grandmother's home.

I think about how if I said all that out loud, Agnes

would get it. Agnes would understand all of this, why it's hard for Maeve to be leaving her house. And then I back up on the bed and look at my grandmother.

"This isn't all about me moving, is it?" asks Maeve in her soft, lilting voice.

I shake my head.

"Change is hard," says Maeve. "And new friends . . . they can be confusing, can't they?"

I nod. I'm a little old for her to be talking to me like this—I'll be twelve in June—but I like her knowing, somehow, without me having to say anything.

"Moving like you did, right in the middle of the year . . . that would make anyone feel out of sorts," she says.

I raise an eyebrow.

"You're not yourself, you make strange choices, things feel like they don't quite fit for a moment," she says. "But it's temporary, Honeypie. You are steadfast."

I shake my head. "No, I'm not." My voice is small.

Then it all floods out in a big rush, right there in the little bedroom with the crystal doorknob: how I love playing with Agnes but maybe I'm too old for it, and how she acts so weird out in public and at school—shouting and walking funny and answering everything in a know-it-all way that no one likes—and how she's gentle and quiet sometimes, like with Billie, and how she was okay just being my after-school friend . . . until I was mean to her.

I was mean to her.

There's no avoiding it, and I don't want to look Maeve in the eye.

But she puts her hand under my chin and makes that happen anyway.

A tear slides down my cheek, and I hear the wail of a siren outside on the street.

"Mattie, you have all the answers already, you know," she says.

"I do?"

"You just laid it out, like a road map of your own heart. That's a pretty special thing to be able to do."

I think back on what I told her. About all the parts of Agnes and the parts of me that fit and don't fit.

"Why is Agnes the way she is?" I ask.

Maeve smiles and looks up at the ceiling, like she's thinking hard about what to say.

"Agnes is special," she says. "She's *extraordinary*. And

it takes a special person to be her friend. Someone who knows that kindness creates confidence."

"But what if my other friends don't see her extraordinariness?"

"Any friend you deem worthy will see the way Agnes shines," says Maeve. "It may take a while, but there's no friend worth having who won't warm up to that lightning bug eventually."

I sigh. This is the kind of advice my parents give, about how real friends are supposed to act. But I don't think kids in sixth grade know that.

"I haven't been a good friend," I tell Maeve. And I thought it would be awful to hear out loud, but it actually feels kind of better once I say it.

"It's not too late to start," says Maeve. "She'll give you another chance. Believe me when I say that as soon as Agnes saw you, she knew you were one of her treasures."

Then she winks.

I never thought of a person as a treasure before, but when I recall my own—the twine ring, the MASH game, the fool's gold—I realize that they're not much by themselves. Other people, people who don't know their stories, don't always see my treasures the same way I do. Because the thing about them is that they're all attached to moments, and *people*, that I want to remember.

I nod at my grandmother, and a lightness comes over me, like I've put down a heavy bag of stuff. And now that Maeve's given me some wisdom, I need to help her too.

"Why didn't anyone tell me you were moving?" I ask, fingering a black string that's coming off the edge of the comforter. And she knows that I'm really asking her why *she* didn't tell me.

"I needed some time," she says. "The truth is that you're right, I didn't want to go at first. Part of me still doesn't. But I need to." She gestures at the tray. "Even getting this up the stairs was hard on my knees."

I look down guiltily.

"The new place is lovely," she says. "I'll have two bedrooms, so you can come and stay, and there's a dining room in my building that's like a fancy restaurant—linen napkins and all. We can wear our gloves."

She's smiling at me so much that I can tell she's faking it a little bit.

"It sounds nice," I say, faking it a little bit too.

"It will be." She touches my nose lightly with her finger. "It's a *transition*, which isn't a bad thing. You know when life stops changing?"

"When?"

"When you're dead!" Maeve smiles at me, a real one, and I grin back. "Now all I need is someone to help me sort my things, figure out what's important . . . what should stay and what should go. Someone who knows me and can identify my true treasures."

"Where will you find a person like that?" I ask, teasing her.

She leans in and hugs me. "Oh, Mattie," she says. "You're wonderful."

I hug her back. I don't feel totally wonderful, but it sounds nice in Maeve's voice. And it makes me want to be that way.

At home that night, Mama and Daddy are both at the dinner table again. Daddy made dinner—his special SpaghettiO Surprise, which is basically canned pasta with some ground turkey and peas mixed in. Mama looks at it like it's a perfect steak, though, and I see them smile at each other.

"She had a good day," says Daddy, and I know he means Maeve. She was all herself today, and she didn't call me Elodie.

"Did she say anything about the move to you, Mattie?" asks Mama while I blow on my steaming-hot forkful of SpaghettiOs.

"Yes," I say. And then, because I assume there'll be a follow-up, I add, "It was between us."

"That's fair," says Daddy.

"But I feel better about it," I say, because I should let them know that things are starting to be more okay.

"I think we all feel better," says Mama, and I notice she's still smiling at Daddy.

Maybe this whole thing—the move up here, new school, new jobs, helping Maeve *transition*—was making everyone unhappy. I think about Mama's chipped nails and Daddy working so much. But then I remember them swaying in the living room and whispering softly, and it makes me feel warm inside.

"We've been out of sorts," I say, and Daddy chuckles.

"That's right, Mathilda *Maeve*." He knows I'm using one of my grandmother's lines.

I go to bed early, feeling good. Because of family stuff, but also because I'm thinking about how I'm going to fix things with Agnes. And I can't wait to get started.

Chapter 25

I wake up the next morning with a mission, and I go to the bathroom to splash some water on my face.

Back in my room, I sit at my corner desk and outline a plan:

> 1. *Apologize to Agnes.*
>
> 2. *Hang out with Agnes over break.*
>   *Activity ideas:*
>   *Billie art*
>   *decorate A's door for Easter*
>   *paint swirls on my walls*
>
> 3. *Find a way to make all my friends like each other*
>   *????*

That last one makes me the most anxious. But I'm not worried about Agnes anymore. She is the way she is. I worry about me, whether I'll be brave enough to be her friend. Whether I'm as wonderful as Maeve says I am. I want to be.

I walk out into the hall to knock on Agnes's door before I even change out of my pajamas.

I do a loud *rat-a-tat-tat* knock. Things are going to be okay. I can feel it.

I hear the padding of Agnes's feet. I know they're hers because they're moving crazy fast. But then they stop. I imagine she's on her tiptoes to look through the peephole.

I give her my best Mattie Maeve Markham megawatt smile, and I wave at the door.

Nothing.

"Agnes?" I call.

"No one's home!" she says, and I hear her scurry away.

My shoulders slump, but just for a moment. I straighten up and go back to my apartment, discouraged but not defeated. Mama makes oatmeal with raisins and brown sugar, and I take my time eating it at the table while I flip through a science magazine.

I'm regrouping.

"What should we do today?" Mama asks.

Suddenly, I realize that she's not at her shift at the bakery. "You don't have work?" I ask hesitantly.

She shakes her head. "This is one of my shifts that got cut," she says. "I've still got a job, but only part-time until business picks up."

"Is that okay?"

"It has to be," she says. She doesn't seem too upset, but I wonder if she's putting on a strong face and she and Daddy are going to start being snippy with each other again. I hope not.

"So, Mattie," Mama tries again. "Do you want to do something together today?"

"I'm busy," I tell her. I'm not being rude or dismissive, just focused.

"Okay, holler if you need anything," she says. "I'll be in the shower."

I sit for a bit longer, and then I walk to the kitchen and rinse out my oatmeal bowl. While I'm wringing the suds from the sponge, it comes to me: an Agnes-worthy idea.

I start by cutting some leftover colored poster board

into two crude shapes that sort of look like girls in dresses. Then I add a few more: hearts, stars, a tiny bird. Mama has a big spotlight that she uses when she takes photos for her baking blog, and she says I can borrow it if I'm careful. So I create a scene right on the glass of the spotlight. I use scotch tape that will come off easily, and I make sure each shape is perfectly placed. When I'm done, the girls in dresses are holding on to the bird together, surrounded by hearts and stars.

"Mattie, that's lovely," says Mama. "Is it for a school project?"

"Kind of," I tell her. I don't want to explain that Agnes gives me light signals on our wall—that's our secret. "It's a picture of friendship."

"I can tell." Mama ruffles my hair and goes to sit at the computer.

Now all I have to do is wait.

The sun moves really slowly when you're wanting it to go down. Especially if you start watching it at eleven a.m. As it creeps across the sky, I do lots of things to entertain myself: games on Mama's phone, a few chapters of the book I got from the school library about an enchanted circus (Agnes would love this one), and an experiment in baking mini red velvet cupcakes with cherries in the middle. Mama mostly did that, but I helped shape the cream cheese frosting into little swirls to top the cupcakes when they were finished. I even finally sharpen the Tar Heel pencil that Finn got for me, and I consider writing him a note for our first day back at school after break, but then I remember that things were weird between us last week, so I don't. I'm focusing on fixing one thing at a time.

And still the sun is up. It's getting to be that golden time, though, when the sky looks yellow pink and any patch of light that gets in through the windows really heats up the room. I lie back in a sun spot on the floor in my bedroom, hands under my head in that universal relaxed stance, and I watch tiny dust particles float around in the sunbeam. Then my brain starts churning.

What am I doing? What if my spotlight plan works and I get Agnes out into the hallway with my signal? Then what? What was I going to say if she opened the door this morning?

I'm not sure. I just know that I want to be face-to-face with her. But maybe I should add more details to my plan.

Mama's in the living room, so I start to practice out loud, but quietly . . . things I might say to Agnes.

"Maybe you could go to more therapy for your weird-ness."

"If you acted a little more normal at school it would be easier for people to be friends with you."

"You act weird sometimes, but I still like you and I hope we can hang out."

Nothing sounds right. So I go simpler.

"You're weird, but it's okay with me and I want to be friends again."

Then I shorten it even more.

"I want to be friends again."

"I miss you."

"Are you okay?"

"I'm sorry."

The shorter I go, the more trouble I have saying the words, even alone in my own room. Why is it that the simplest sentences are the hardest to say out loud?

"What are you doing, sweets?" Mama's in the door-way.

"Practicing," I tell her.

She smiles. "That last one sounded good."

Mama knows things.

I hear the front door open.

"Daddy's home," she says. "Come have dinner."

We sit down to eat, and Mama and Daddy talk about his day at work and her red velvet experiment. He tells her he's proud that even when she has a day off she's working on the blog and getting things going. "I try," she says, and he looks at her with heart eyes. I see them. They start to talk about adult-life stuff then, which isn't so interesting and is maybe even a little scary, but while they do it they open up a bottle of wine and clink glasses. I raise my apple juice into the mix because I like the sound. I like the tone of their voices too, easy and bright. But I don't really listen to the details of their conversation—I'm distracted. Because all the while it's getting darker and darker.

Finally, after I watch a cooking competition show and change into pajamas and brush my teeth, I'm ready. I take the spotlight into my room and close the door.

I position the light in my window and plug it in. Immediately, the friendship scene I created—the girls, the bird, the hearts and stars—lights up the brick wall outside. The sharp lines of the shadows look even better than I thought they would. . . . There's no missing this signal. As I stare at the scene, I think about how much has happened since I moved here just a few months ago.

My own heartbeat sounds louder than usual. I'm nervous. I have no way of knowing if Agnes's shades are up or down, if she's in her room or even home at all. I could bang on the wall, but I want to give it time. She'll signal back, won't she? If she sees it.

I wait impatiently, more waiting, and after a few minutes I open my window. It's chilly out, but not awful, and I want to see if I can hear anything from Agnes's apartment. At first the only sound is the wind.

And then I see it, right above my scene . . . Agnes's shining star.

It goes dark after a few seconds, but it was there.

"Be right back!" I say to Mama and Daddy as I walk through the living room to get out the door. I hear Daddy say, "What?" but Mama shushes him. She knows things.

Agnes is already in the hallway.

"Hi," she says.

"Hey," I say. And suddenly I wish I'd brought props

like she did on New Year's Eve, or at least some sparkling water to share. I don't know what to do with my hands.

Agnes sits down against the hallway wall, so I sit next to her.

"I liked your signal," she says. And I'm grateful. Because it feels like she's already starting to forgive me.

"I'm sorry about . . . ," I start. But then I stop. *Keep it simple.* "I'm sorry."

Agnes smiles the kind of smile that comes right before you start crying, and when a tear falls I'm not sure if she's happy or sad. I begin to pull at the dark-blue carpet— there's a tuft that's coming undone under my fingers.

"Are we friends?" asks Agnes. And it's a question that makes sense to me, finally, because she's not asking if we can go back to the way we were, as afternoon friends who don't talk at school. She means are we friends for real— the type of friends who don't have rules.

"Yes," I say. And I look her in the eye when I say it. She's not looking back, not at first, but then she raises her head and her brown eyes meet mine. "We're friends," I say, to confirm it.

"We're just us, and we're okay," she says.

"We're just us," I repeat. "And we're friends."

I see her face soften, and then Agnes does something totally unexpected.

She opens her arms, and it's a quick one, all bony arms and weird angles, but it's unmistakable. It's a hug.

Chapter 26

Mrs. Davis came over for dinner last night, and she and Agnes told us that Mr. Davis is staying in Boston.

"They're getting divorced," said Agnes, and that made Mama pause mid-potato pass.

But Mrs. Davis smiled at Agnes and said, "Thanks for saying it for me."

And Agnes said, "Mom has trouble with the D word, but my therapist, Lisa, says it's good to talk about it."

"Lisa's right," says Mrs. Davis. Then she shares a glance with my mom. "Agnes is way ahead of me on this one . . . and lots of other things."

I watch Mama give her soft eyes that understand. I want to practice that look in the mirror. I also want to know more about this therapist now that it's out in the open.

"Do you like Lisa?" I ask Agnes. She did bring it up, after all.

"Yeah," she says. "She's helping me cope with my anxiety."

I nod and smile, trying to do Mama's soft-eyed look. I think I get it pretty well because Agnes meets my eyes and smiles back.

Mrs. Davis doesn't say anything that makes me feel weird, like that I'm more important than Agnes's therapist, and later, after we offer to clear the dishes, I tell Agnes that I'm sorry about the divorce.

"It's okay," she says, going into her robot voice again. "Mom and I have been here together. Nothing is different. Dad likes Boston, and now I have two places to be."

I think the robot voice means that Agnes is repeating what she's been told, and that's okay. It helps her, just like the smiling-to-make-yourself-happy trick Maeve taught me for when I'm nervous.

★ ★ ★

Now it's Saturday on the last weekend of spring break, and Agnes and I are painting big blue polka dots on the wall behind my bed. Mama helped us move the mattress, desk, and dresser to the center of the room, and Agnes brought over a drop cloth for the floor. Turns out her left-over blue, called Peacock, goes really well with my golden Wonderstruck walls.

"These can be like thought bubbles or dream clouds," says Agnes, and that's just how I was thinking about them. Like my own curiosity rising up above my sleeping head onto the wall. Maybe the bubbles will even carry away my worries—some of them are fading already, like the ones about Mama and Daddy fighting, and the one about Agnes.

"So I have something to tell you about Maeve," I say. I haven't wanted to talk to anyone about my grandmother moving, really. I think part of me is pretending it won't happen. But somehow I'm ready to tell Agnes.

"What?" asks Agnes, and she stops painting, like she's nervous.

When I say it, I can see her lip tremble. Agnes knows

it means that the house, the place where all the treasures are and where Maeve has lived for more years than I can even imagine, will be gone forever.

"That's sad, Mattie," she says.

"I know." Somehow, even just telling Agnes makes it feel better. She's sharing the sad part with me now.

Suddenly, though, Agnes brightens. "Don't worry. We'll make sure Maeve's treasures don't disappear."

"How?"

"I have an idea," says Agnes. But she doesn't tell me what it is. She changes the subject.

"Has Shari seen your room?" she asks, and I get a nervous tickle inside.

"No. She hasn't been here."

"Maybe we should invite her over," says Agnes.

I get quiet. This week has been really fun. Agnes and I wrote messages to each other with her invisible ink set, pretending we were detectives solving a murder case. We followed footprints we discovered outside in the gardens to find out who'd been walking on the grounds where they shouldn't, and we tracked them to . . . Sam, the grounds guy who handles the window boxes on the first floor. We also decorated Agnes's door with shiny wrapping paper cut into Easter eggs, baked brownies in the shapes of animals, and blew giant bubbles out her living room windows into the courtyard below, which made people look up at us like we were magicians.

I keep painting, filling in the blue circle on my wall until it gets darker and darker. Even though I want Agnes and Shari to be friends, I'm not ready to attempt it, like, today.

"I think Shari's still on vacation," I finally say.

"Oh," says Agnes. Then she pauses and holds up her paintbrush. "But one day let's show her what we do."

I smile and nod. "Okay," I say. And I mean it. I *will* try. But I can't help wondering if Agnes and school friends will ever work.

I realize that Easter at Maeve's may be the last holiday we have in her old house. But when I get there and rush into her Shalimar-scented hug, I remember that it's not the house that's the treasure—it's my grandmother.

Elodie and Aunt Cindy and Uncle Jay drove in for the holiday weekend; they've been staying at Maeve's, so it's a full house, and Agnes is here with her mom too. We invited them to come with us, since an Easter table set for two didn't seem festive enough.

My cousin greets Agnes and me coolly at first—she's like that—but when Agnes finishes the scavenger hunt Maeve set up for our Easter baskets in under twenty minutes, Elodie gives her a look of respect.

"She's a clue genius," Elodie whispers to me, and all I can do is nod in agreement.

When we sit down at the table, Maeve pats the chair next to her. "For Lightning Bug," she says, and I have a feeling . . .

Yup! Immediately Agnes picks up her knife to see if it rattles—and it does. My grandmother may be forgetting stuff, but not the important things.

We eat ham and creamed spinach and green beans and sweet potatoes with marshmallow fluff before we're allowed to tear into our Easter basket candy. Maeve got a special basket for Agnes, and it has another one of the marble eggs in it—a purple one. Agnes holds it up to the light like it's the most beautiful thing she's ever seen. "Are you sure?" she asks Maeve.

"Those eggs are heavy," says Maeve with a wink. "I've got too many of them to carry in the move. Do me a favor and lighten the load."

Agnes smiles at Maeve, and I see Elodie watching them too.

Later, Agnes gets out an orange pen and her spiral-bound notebook and walks very slowly around Maeve's house. When she starts up the stairs, I open my mouth to ask her what she's doing, but before any sound even comes out, she turns and says, "Treasure list." I know just what she means, so I let her go.

When Aunt Cindy and Uncle Jay pack up their car to head back to Vermont, I give Elodie a hug good-bye and she whispers to me, "Your friend is cool."

I know she doesn't mean it in the regular way, like the kind of cool you'd call a popular girl. Elodie means it in an even better way. She means core cool, like underneath it all. And my cousin noticing that makes me feel a little better about facing school tomorrow with Agnes. Which is good, because I know that this part of my plan is going to be the hardest.

Chapter 27

I knock on Agnes's door at 8:10 a.m., just like I said I would, and we take the elevator down to the lobby. She's carrying a big sculpture she made of Billie the bird, and it's covered in bubble wrap. We wave to Doorman Will and push open the double doors with our backs at the same time, stepping into the yellow April morning.

I don't hesitate when I see Marisa's lip turn up at the sight of us. I don't meet her ice-blue eyes, even though I can feel her staring. I think about how she's probably still sad about her parents splitting up, how maybe she had a hard morning. And although I can't quite bring myself to smile at her, I don't let her stare get to me.

"Hi, Finn! Is that for me?" Marisa's voice is bright and loud behind us, and I resist the urge to turn and look at them to see what she's talking about. Maybe he brought her a present from his trip to North Carolina, which might make me upset later but not right now. My face is relaxed. I'm standing with Agnes.

"No, it's for someone else," he says.

Agnes and I both spin to face him.

"Hi, Finn," Agnes says first.

He looks surprised, but he smiles at her.

"Hi," he says.

Then he turns to me, holding out a small, wrapped box. "This is for you, Tar Heel."

I reach out and open it before I can tremble, but I feel the tremble coming. And when I lift up the box top and see a tiny little gold necklace in the shape of my old home state, I almost feel like crying in the good way.

"What's this for?" I ask him.

"We visited my uncle over break," says Finn. "I spent a lot of time at the mall."

I raise my eyebrows. That still doesn't really explain it.

"It made me think of you," he says, reaching out to lift

it from the box. "Want to wear it?"

I nod, glad to have a reason to turn my back to him as my face turns red. He opens up the clasp, and I pull my hair around to one side as he reaches around my neck to fasten the chain in the back. I let out a quiet sigh before I steady myself and face him again.

"Thank you," I say.

"Treasure," whispers Agnes. She's standing close to us.

"What?" asks Finn.

"She just means it's really cool," I say, and Agnes nods up and down, up and down really fast.

Finn smiles. "I'm glad you both like it."

When we get on the bus, Agnes and I sit together in a seat behind Finn. Marisa slides in next to him, but he turns to talk to us the whole time. She faces forward, and I can sense anger vibrating off her. I *almost* feel bad about it.

The bus ride gives me more confidence. Agnes and Finn are talking, sort of. At least through me. He asks about the bubble wrap, and Agnes tells him it's a sculpture of the baby bird. "Want to help us set it up in Mr. Perl's room?" I ask him, and he nods. Agnes raises her hand in a *stop* motion, and for a second I get nervous—what if she screams or shouts that it's not okay?—but then she says, "Finn can carry Billie. She's heavy!" and we all break up laughing.

By the time the morning is starting and everyone is filing into class, Agnes has talked more to Finn than I have. They both know a lot about the *How to Train Your Dragon* movies, so they've been reciting lines by heart while I stay out of it. "I've seen those, like, twice!" I say when they sniff at my lack of knowledge.

I'm starting to feel comfortable, sort of, but when Shari walks into the room, I can see the question on her face, even though she doesn't ask it: *Why are you guys with her?*

"Mattie!" She rushes up to hug me and she's all hand gestures and hair—her long braids are back and she has "a million stories" about the Bahamas. "You would not believe how blue the water is—it's almost green," she says. "And I got to touch a dolphin, which felt like rubber, and there were six waterslides and one was really really tall but I went down it anyway and it never rained and the ocean felt like a bath and my dad even let me pull the handle on a slot machine and I won forty-two dollars!"

"It sounds amazing!" I say, and then I see that Agnes is standing really close to us. Shari gives her a curious look, and when she asks how my break was, I turn to include Agnes. "It was great! Agnes and I painted my room in this really cool way that you'd love. Plus, we baked delicious brownies and made up detective games and did a bunch of art projects." I'm talking so fast that I'm not giving myself time to see how Shari's responding, but I can tell that Agnes is smiling a mile wide and nodding along with what I'm saying and I feel like I'm finally being wonderful, or at least better.

When I pause for a breath, Agnes herself jumps in. "Shari, you should come hang out with us at Butler Towers. There are doormen and an elevator, and we could even go up to the roof maybe to see the whole town. I bet we could see your house from there."

And I almost want to side-hug her for trying.

But Shari crinkles up her face like she's not sure what to say, like she doesn't understand why we're talking to Agnes. Why *she's* talking to Agnes.

Then Mr. Perl asks us all to take our seats, and my heart is pounding hard because I don't know if this is working.

The morning lesson starts, and Shari and I don't get to talk more. When the bell rings for lunch, we usually walk out together to meet Robin and Emily. Today, I wait for Agnes.

"Want to sit with us?" I ask.

"Yes!" She does the nodding-up-and-down thing again.

Shari doesn't say anything, but that means she doesn't say no.

At the table, Emily and Robin give Shari a questioning look when Agnes puts down her tray, and I see Shari shrug.

Agnes digs in, eating fast and furious.

Everyone is really quiet.

Agnes vacuums up her food in about two minutes, and then she says, "I need to go talk to Mr. Perl about something."

"Okay, see you later," I say, and she bolts from the table.

My stomach tightens. I wanted this to be easier for me. For Agnes. It was brave of her to sit with us for the first time, and I didn't help her fit in.

"What's the deal?" asks Robin, and when I look at her face, it doesn't quite look mad, just confused.

"Yeah," says Emily. "She is super weird."

"I know. . . ." I'm not sure what to say. I didn't practice for this part. But I remember how Maeve said that kindness creates confidence. And so I'm thinking of all the things I like about Agnes, and I'm about to speak up, but then I hear Shari.

"I think . . . ," she starts. "I think Mattie is friends with Agnes. Maybe she has been for a while?"

She looks at me, like she's waiting for me to confirm that. And there's a moment where it seems like I'm walking on a fence, and if I deny this, I'll fall back into my friendships with these girls, who welcomed me as the new kid this year. But if I jump the other way, if I say that yes, I *am* friends with Agnes, I'm not sure where I'll land. And I may land alone.

I open my mouth to speak—I know what I need to

do—when Marisa breezes by our table. "Finally eating with your best friend?"

She's staring right at me and her face looks mean, as usual, but I notice something else too. She looks pathetic. Like she has nothing better to do at lunch than walk by and start something with me. It's sad.

"Yeah," I say. "Agnes is my friend. We spend a lot of time together, actually."

Marisa smiles smugly as she looks at Robin, Emily, and Shari with triumphant eyes.

But they're not looking at her. They're looking at me. Waiting.

"Agnes is definitely weird," I say to them. "But weird isn't bad. She's really smart, for one."

I see Shari nod slightly, and that gives me courage to go on.

"Also, she's fun. She lives next door to me, and her door is always decorated for whatever holiday is next in this really elaborate way," I say. "Like she made shamrocks for St. Patrick's Day and George Washington's head for Presidents' Day—"

"What about Abraham Lincoln?" Robin chimes in,

and when I look at her I see she's smiling. Maybe she's about to make fun of Agnes, so I barrel over her because I think that sometimes if you keep going in the right direction, people will come along.

"His too!" I say. I'm on a roll now. "And she's so creative—you guys should see her room. It's full of rainbows and the best kind of crazy stuff. Her design philosophy is that a space should be 'an ordered collection of magic and wonder.'" I do air quotes.

Emily laughs. "I like that."

I can feel Marisa fuming at the end of the table, but I don't even turn to look at her. She walks away silently, and Emily rolls her eyes. "Marisa's so mean," she says.

Shari is still looking right at me, and her expression is hard to read. Is she mad? Confused? She looks away before I can tell.

Then Robin starts talking about how they changed the theme song to her favorite TV show, and Emily wonders why the best YouTube makeup star hasn't done a new video in, like, two weeks. Our lunch table returns to normal, and I don't bring up Agnes again. That's enough for now.

Soon the bell is ringing to send us back to class. When Shari and I walk down the hallway to Mr. Perl's room, she slows down before we get to the door. "Why didn't you tell me about Agnes?" she asks quietly as we stop walking.

Her eyes are on the floor, so I look down there too. Staring into the sparkle of her purple sequined Vans, I know I need to tell the truth.

"I was afraid to," I say.

"Why?"

Her head picks up, and so I lift my eyes too. "I thought maybe you'd think I was weird. Or you wouldn't want to be my friend."

She looks annoyed. "I'm not a mean person," she says.

"I know!" I say. "I didn't think that. . . . It's just . . . Agnes is so different."

She takes a deep breath. "Yeah," she says. "But I still wish you'd told me."

Then she turns and walks into the classroom, and Agnes is there sitting at her desk already. I see Shari wave to her, and Agnes lights up, giving a big smile and a huge wave back.

I slink into my seat, feeling both proud and icky. Because I think I'm doing the right thing, but maybe it is too late.

Shari doesn't whisper funny things to me that afternoon like she usually does while Mr. Perl teaches. Agnes has to go home early today for a doctor's appointment—I know it's an added therapy session, and I give her a big wave and smile when she quietly leaves class. Bryce notices and squints up his eyes like, *What is going on?* But he doesn't say anything.

The bell rings, and this is a time when Shari and I always wait for each other to get our stuff in order and walk out to the bus circle together. Today, though, she hurriedly packs up her backpack and starts walking out.

But then I see her stop just inside the door. She doesn't turn around, but it still feels like she's giving me a chance.

I walk up behind her. "I'm sorry," I say, and I feel the wonder of those two words. They come easier this time.

Shari nods, and then she starts walking. She's going slowly, staying by my side. When we get out to the bus circle, she bumps me from the side. "I knew you were weird from the first day you walked into class, by the way," she says, giving me a small sideways grin. "Being normal is so boring anyway."

Chapter 28

The smell of sugar and lemons fills Blue Sky Bakery as Shari, Agnes, and I slide into a booth by the big window.

"Okay, girls, I'm trying out a new recipe—sugar cookies with citrus," says Mama as she emerges from the kitchen. She sets up three plates for us with lemon-shaped cookies that have sparkling yellow-and-green sprinkles on them.

When I told Mama that I wanted to have Shari and Agnes hang out together, she suggested she show us the bakery, and she picked us all up at school.

Agnes has been eating lunch at our table every day

this week. She's mostly quiet, which is okay, but when she talks everyone seems to listen to what she has to say, even when what she has to say is weird, which it just is sometimes. That's Agnes.

"Mmm . . . ," says Shari after she takes a bite of the cookie.

"Really good, Mama," I tell her. All of her recipes are yummy, but something about this one is extra delicious.

"The touch of sour makes the sweetness stand out even more, Mrs. Markham!" says Agnes after she finishes her cookie in three quick bites.

Mama claps her hands together. "That's just what I was hoping, Agnes!"

Shari's looking kind of sideways at Agnes, but when I catch her eye and smile at her she grins back and it doesn't feel like we're making fun of Agnes, more like we're *appreciating* her, as Maeve would say.

I know Shari still thinks Agnes is weird—I can tell by the way she pauses after Agnes says something especially random—but she's also definitely giving her a chance, and that's all I can ask for. I have to believe that, at some point, Shari will see how much fun Agnes can be.

A man with a big mustache walks out from the back and stops by our table. "Who do we have here?" he asks.

"Bob, this is my daughter, Mattie, and her friends Agnes and Shari," says Mama. "Girls, this is Mr. Brown. He owns the bakery."

We all smile, but it's Agnes who speaks up. "Mr. Brown, Mrs. Markham makes the best cookies I've ever tasted," she says.

"Well, I—" Mr. Brown starts, but Agnes isn't done talking.

"She knows how to combine savory and sweet, and everything she makes is so pretty too!"

Shari and I nod in agreement, and Mr. Brown laughs in one loud burst. "You're not wrong, Agnes!" he says. "She's a talented baker."

He gives us a wave and goes back to the kitchen. Mama follows. "Holler if you need anything, girls," she calls over her shoulder. "I'll just be a few minutes."

"What's the matter, Mattie?" Agnes asks when they're both gone.

"Nothing," I say.

"You're frowning," says Shari, and I know I am.

I poke at the silver napkin holder for a minute, making the napkins squish in and out with a *clink-clink* sound.

"My mom only has part-time hours, but I think she needs to work more," I whisper. "For money."

"But it seems like Bob Brown loves her," Shari says, and Agnes nods up and down, up and down.

"Yeah, but look around," I say, turning my head to take in the entire bakery, which is almost half a block long, with lots of booths and four shiny silver display counters for sweets. "We're the only people here."

My friends follow my gaze.

"That's true," says Shari, her voice dropping. But then she brightens up. "I know! I'll tell my mom about this place. She's so into sugar that she made us go all the way to New York City for a cupcake once."

"Thanks," I say. But I can't help thinking that Shari bringing in her mom isn't going to make much difference.

"It's so pretty here," says Agnes, taking in the high arched ceiling covered in white tiles and the metal lights hanging down to spotlight the treats.

"I know." I sigh. "It's like a party room."

I feel Agnes and Shari both look at me quickly. I meet

their eyes, which are sparkling like mine all of a sudden. "You guys . . . ," I say. And I know we're thinking the same thing.

Over the next few weekends, Agnes comes with me and Daddy to Maeve's on Saturdays. She brings her flip-top notebook and her orange pen, and we add items to the Treasure List each time—the blue Danish Christmas plates, the Virgin Mary Lladró statue, the tiger's-eye marble set in the purple velvet box. Agnes and I do an especially careful job packing up Maeve's boxes, and today is our last Saturday here. But instead of feeling sad, I feel excited. Because Agnes's special idea for Maeve's treasures? She finally shared it with me—and it's good.

"Attention, attention!" I call to my grandmother and my dad as Agnes rings the brass bell hanging in the entryway. They come in from having coffee in the dining room and sit on the red couch, which is pretty much the last piece of furniture standing in this room—the movers arrive on Monday.

"We have an announcement," I say.

"I should hope so, with that noise," says Maeve, but

her eyes are twinkling. "What is it, my doves?"

I look at Agnes. It was her idea, so she gets to tell.

"You may notice that four of these boxes have blue stars on them," she says, pointing like a game show host to the special packing we did, complete with signature doodles. "That is because they won't be going to Maeve's new apartment this week."

"They won't?" asks Daddy, but I put my finger to my lips to shush him. Agnes has the floor.

"They won't," she says. "Instead, we're taking Maeve's treasures to Mr. Bennington at the Germantown Historical Society."

"Mr. Bennington?" Daddy always takes a minute to catch on, but Maeve is already smiling.

Agnes opens the box we left unsealed for dramatic purposes. She pulls out a tiny travel clock that Maeve bought on a trip to Spain and Morocco when she was nineteen. Its face is yellowed, but it still works, and the numbers are shaped with swirly edges. It has a quiet tick.

"For this one, we might tell the story of an evening in Morocco . . . ," Agnes says. Then she looks to me.

"Picture it: the nineteen fifties. Northern Africa. A

young girl sleeps too late. . . ."

Maeve claps her hands together in delight. "She stops by a market in Tangier, where she finds a clock that looks like it belongs in a genie bottle. She doesn't know to bargain, but the young man who's selling it offers her half off if she'll come to a dance with him that evening. . . ."

"Mother!" My dad interrupts, but he's grinning.

Agnes and I giggle into our hands. Maeve gets it. She can tell the story of each object to Mr. Bennington, and he can use a few for his exhibit on the lives and travels of longtime Philadelphians.

"Mr. Bennington wants to meet with you this week," I tell her. "Agnes set it up." According to Mrs. Davis, that means she took Agnes by the museum to "talk Mr. Bennington's ear off until he said yes."

Agnes doesn't say anything, but her smile is like a giant half-moon.

And so is Maeve's.

Chapter 29

By the last week of the competition, Agnes's team is way ahead in trivia, probably because since we've fixed things between us, she hasn't missed a single day. Maybe her extra therapy is helping, but I like to think it's also me. Agnes taught Shari and me a trick to buzz in more quickly—it involved a wrist motion that you wouldn't believe—and even Bryce gave her an approving nod after that. But she was still faster.

When Mr. Perl announces that Team One gets to decide where the end-of-school party will be next week, Agnes's hand shoots up.

"Agnes?"

"Yes, Mr. Perl," she says, standing up to address everyone. "We already know where we want to have the party." She's looking right at me, and my palms get sweaty.

My leg starts bouncing up and down, but Finn touches my knee under the desk to still it, and that makes my face get red. He pulls his hand away, and when I look at him, his face is getting red too. He knows about our plan.

"This year, we've decided to hold the end-of-school party at Blue Sky Bakery in downtown Philadelphia," says Agnes.

I look around to see the class reaction; everyone is still and quiet.

"The theme is Sweet Victory, and there will be lots of treats!" she continues.

Mr. Perl laughs. "What a tasty thought, Agnes."

Then I see it—people are smiling and nodding. They like our idea!

At the bakery, Agnes, Shari, and I had hatched a plan to convince Team One that Blue Sky was the perfect spot for the party. The plan had three phases. Here's how it went down:

Phase One: I told my mom I had to bring in snacks

for a school thing (not a lie), so she baked a bunch of her classic chocolate chip oatmeal cookies and Agnes and I wrapped them up into four little bags. She gave them to her team members the next day "to celebrate our soon-to-be win" and casually mentioned that she got them at Blue Sky Bakery downtown.

Phase Two: We knew that one of Agnes's team members, Ari Dwyer, had been talking about wanting to have the party at Rick's Minigolf if they won the trivia contest. So one day at lunch, Shari announced very loudly that she'd been minigolfing that weekend and she saw a mouse pop its head out of one of the holes. Another Team One member, Isabella Blau, shrieked in disgust. That crossed Rick's off the list.

Phase Three: In the cafeteria line the next day, Robin and I got right behind Ari Dwyer. He was annoyed that his minigolf idea was nixed, so when Robin started talking excitedly about how she *had* to have her birthday at Blue Sky Bakery next year because it was so huge and fancy and obviously the best place ever for a party, we could practically see the lightbulb go on over Ari's head.

By the time we were done with the members of Team

One, they thought the bakery was *their* idea! All Agnes had to do when Ari proposed it was nod along with everyone else on her team.

A bonus of this plan? Shari and Agnes and I got to brainstorm a caper together, and that was good for my goal of them becoming something like friends.

"Everyone, a round of applause for Team One, the clear winner of this year's trivia extravaganza!" says Mr. Perl.

When the claps start, I join in and my face is in a full-on beam.

The second-to-last day of school is a half day, and our class party is in the afternoon. A field-trip bus takes us downtown, and Blue Sky Bakery is gleaming when we walk in. The silver counters are lined with small bites of Mama's lemon sugar cookies, magic bars, French-style macarons, and swirly rainbow cupcakes with fairy frosting. A bunch of parents are here—even Daddy, who took part of the afternoon off work.

"Step right up, step right up!" Agnes is acting like a circus ringmaster, directing people to different counters and describing the samples Mama made. Every time she talks about a treat, she adds, "Baked by the famous Liz Markham!" and she's shouting so loudly that I know Bob Brown hears her. He's walking around the bakery with a giant grin plastered on his face, and he keeps turning to look back at the register when it dings to ring up a parent's purchase. The samples are free, but people are buying lots to take home.

I slide into a booth across from Shari, and I see her grin over my shoulder.

"They're coming," she whispers, and a second later, Finn scoots in next to me and Bryce is jostling Shari to get her to make room.

"Don't be a booth hog," he says, and she rolls her eyes and clicks her tongue at him, but I know what's underneath.

It's the same feeling I have now that Finn's so close to me, and when he reaches below the table and moves to position his hand over mine, I feel like my heart might stop. So I stare out the window for a second until I can make my breathing normal again.

Then I look back at him to smile, but I see Marisa

heading toward us, and I tense up, expecting her to drop some sort of mean-bomb like she always does.

When she gets to the end of our booth she says, "Your mom's cookies are really good." She's looking down at the table and not at anyone in particular, but obviously that comment was meant for me.

"Thanks," I say, and when she raises her gaze, her blue eyes don't look at all like ice.

Before I can second-guess myself, I say, "Do you want to sit down?"

She smiles a little and pulls up a chair to sit at the end, and it reminds me of the sore-thumb fifth desk in our classroom setup, which didn't turn out to be such a bad arrangement for me after all.

Then Bryce and Shari start arguing about which dessert sample is the best, and Finn shows us how to make a paper straw wrapper into a wiggling worm with drops of water. Marisa stays pretty quiet, which is the right move. I see her smile a few times and nod along with us while we talk. I think she's practicing her soft eyes.

By the time the party's over, I don't know if it's all the sugar that has me feeling shaky or the fact that Finn stays near me all day and holds my hand under the table at the booth for a really long time. I don't want to let go, but eventually I have to use the bathroom. I think we'll hold hands again, though. Soon. Preferably somewhere farther away from my parents.

As people file out of the bakery to go home, there's a low rumble of everyone making summer plans. Even though we'll see one another for the last day of school tomorrow, today feels like the end of the year. Then Agnes runs up to our booth and tells us that Mr. Perl ate four minicupcakes. "I counted!" she says.

I see Mama behind the counter with Bob Brown, and they're both smiling and nodding. Daddy is across the room talking to someone's mom, but I watch him look over at Mama a few times, and every time he does it's like his face has this inside glow. He's proud of her.

I think if all the parents follow up with coming to the bakery over the summer and telling their friends how great it is, it's possible that Mama will get her full-time hours back. But even if she doesn't—and she has to look for a new job or whatever—I can tell by how Daddy's smiling at her, like she's the only person in this whole big space, that our family will be okay.

After everyone clears out and Daddy goes back to the office, I wait with Mama to clean up. Finn, Shari, and Agnes stay too. Agnes was already planning to ride home with us, but Finn and Shari just offer to help us clear out the sample trays and sweep, so Bob Brown puts them to work and Mama tells them to call their parents—she'll drive them home. She knows things.

As we walk out to our car, it's still bright outside, and Agnes says, "I love long summer days," which is just what I was thinking, and Mama says, "Should we bring some of these extra cookies over to Maeve's?"

I pause, but before I can worry about Maeve meeting Shari and Finn in her new place, Agnes says, "That's a great idea—you guys will love Maeve!" And, amazingly, Agnes gives me confidence.

When we get to her door, Maeve seems happy to see all of us. After Finn walks inside, my grandmother gives me wiggle-eyebrows behind his back, and I rush in to hug her for two reasons: 1) I love hugging Maeve, and 2) I need to be sure Finn doesn't turn around and see her being goofy.

"I'm living a life of leisure now!" Maeve tells us, as if her days have changed so much in this new place. She demonstrates how her recliner has seven different positions, and she lets us sit in the big porch swing on her patio. I'm still getting used to her apartment—it's really different, but it has a white fluffy rug and it already smells like Shalimar.

Shari and Finn and I stay outside on the patio and kick our feet to make the swing rock while we talk about summer plans. Finn's neighborhood has a pool and he says Bryce comes a lot and we can also use his guest passes anytime, which makes me think about him in a bathing suit and maybe splashing around in the water and possibly even hanging out all day, and I get this happy feeling in my chest like there's a bright sun spot hitting me and warming up my insides.

When I turn back and look through the sliding glass doors, I see Mama straightening up Maeve's kitchen and Agnes sitting with Maeve on the red couch. They're flipping through a photo album.

"Excuse me for a sec," I say to Shari and Finn, and I step into the living room. Maeve is showing Agnes a photo of herself as an eight-year-old in a flowing butterfly costume with long brown ringlets. I know this one—it's from a church play she did back in West Virginia.

Maeve is speaking softly, remembering, and Agnes is paying careful attention to my grandmother's voice, and for a moment it feels like everything is going to be fine. Even better than fine.

A few minutes later, after a few more photos and memories shared, Shari and Finn come inside and the room gets louder and Agnes says she wants to look for the tissue paper we used to wrap the marble eggs.

She finds it in a box in the corner and then she asks Maeve for scissors. And when my grandmother looks confused, Agnes says, "Oh, you just unpacked! How could you know where they are?" and she goes on a hunt on her own and finds them in a kitchen drawer.

Then Agnes shows Shari and Finn and me how to make big puffy flowers and tiny little butterflies out of the tissue paper.

When we leave, Maeve's door is the prettiest in the hall, if not in the whole building—it looks like a butterfly garden.

★ ★ ★

Mama snapped a photo of Shari, Agnes, Finn, and me sitting across Maeve's porch swing that day, and later she ordered two prints of it. Agnes and I crafted frames with stick-on jewels and painted butterflies. One was for Maeve, who had a little trouble remembering who Shari and Finn were but knew "Lightning Bug" right away.

The other framed photo went right up on my windowsill, the first treasure from my new home.

And you know what? It looks like it's been there forever.

Acknowledgments

Thanks are in order because even though writing a book can be a solitary venture—and this one in particular was written very quietly—there are always lots of people around who keep me going, even when they don't know it.

To my dear departed grandmother Carol, who may have had a soft, southern whisper and a row house in Philadelphia and marble eggs and the ability to make magic real.

To my parents, who gave me the experience of moving and changing schools and therefore made me very upset, but also made me a more adaptable human. Or at least gave me access to the tangled emotions that make good writing fodder.

To Sophia Sonny, who takes care of my children with

such affection and know-how that I can spend time writing in cafes all over Brooklyn.

To Micol Ostow, Morgan Baden, Sarah MacLean, and Lauren Mechling for reading early drafts of this "I think maybe it's a middle grade?" draft and telling me I should keep going, along with some sharp feedback.

To my agent, Doug Stewart, who is extremely deft at identifying tiny tweaks that don't take much work on my part but make the books I write infinitely better. This is a quality I love!

To Jen Klonsky, whom I've admired from afar for years—I'm so thrilled to be working with such a smart, insightful editor. And to Catherine Wallace, who made the finishing touches process easy and breezy.

To production editor Alexandra Rakaczki and designer Alison Klapthor, who made everything go smoothly while keeping the process exciting (a good combo). And to Lucy Truman, who captured the characters so well in her cover illustration that I keep finding new, small details to adore (look again!).

To the publicity and marketing teams at HarperCollins, especially Stephanie Hoover and Megan Barlog, for sharing the book to reaches of the reading world that are beyond my scope.

And always to Dave, June, and Ida Lou, who are my home.

Turn the page for a
sneak peek of

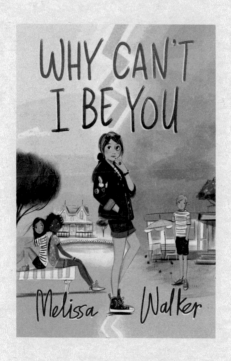

Chapter 1

Whem I reach underneath my bed to look for Ronan's Transformer, here is what I find:

Dust balls. People sometimes call them "bunnies," but that doesn't make sense to me. They're balls, or maybe floating masses. But bunnies? No.

A red plastic spear, which could be mistaken for a toothpick. I know, however, that it's the broken end of Darth Vader's lightsaber from my six-year-old birthday cake topper.

A puzzle piece with blue flowers on it.

That last thing makes me go *oh!*, because it's my mom's. She does puzzles and then glues them together and frames them. They're all over our walls. And this particular puzzle, with blue hydrangeas, has been missing its last piece for almost a year.

I stick it in my back pocket—Mom will be so happy.

"Can't find it!" I shout to Ronan as I head out the screen door and onto our tiny square of porch where he's waiting in the plastic lawn chair.

"Well, keep an eye out," he says with a scowl.

"What do you need it for anyway?" I ask him. We're eleven now, and I don't think he plays Transformers anymore. Does he?

"It's lucky," he mumbles.

"What?" I'm not sure I heard him right.

"I just want it back. Okay, Claire?" he says, his face softening a little as he closes his eyes to the bright June sunlight. Ronan's freckles are just starting to show on his pale skin as the summer sun gets more intense, and his sandy-brown hair is growing longer, shaggy. It looks good that way, like how boys on TV wear theirs.

I wonder if the Transformer search has anything to do with his father being back, but I don't ask.

"Anyway."

He says that word a lot lately with nothing to follow it. Like "anyway" means something. Still he stays, unmoving, in the chair on our porch square, so I think he wants to talk more.

I sit down on the top step to wait, since there's only the one chair and our porch isn't big enough for both of us, which is one of the reasons why "porch" is a generous word. I think you have to be able to fit two seats in an area for it to be called something as sociable as a porch.

I pick at the strings on the edges of my jean shorts as I wait for Ronan to talk, because he will . . . eventually. It's the start of summer break, and our moms are at work; he tends to talk when there is no one else around but me.

This is the first summer I'm allowed to stay home alone. Last year I went to a YMCA camp because Mom helps clean the gym on Saturdays, but it was a lot of craft-making and running drills, neither of which are my thing. I only really like the court time—basketball is my favorite sport. In a couple of years I'll be old enough to be a counselor-in-training, which Mom wants me to do, but I figured out a way to convince her to let me stay home this summer.

"I've heard that free time is really good for kids," I told Mom. And then I quoted a poster that was in my guidance counselor's office last year: "'How can I be curious if I don't have time to dream?'"

"My little girl is almost twelve." Mom had let out this low sigh, and then she looked at me with her mushy emotional face and I knew she was saying yes. This summer is my moment between going to kids' camp and having to do more grown-up working stuff. I turn twelve in August. So does Ronan. Our birthdays are three days apart, actually. And we live next door to each other in Twin Pines Trailer Park.

"Are you going to Brianna's party?" Ronan asks after a long silence.

"Yeah," I say. "Her new house has a pool, so it's a pool party! Jealous?"

"I'm going too," he says, sitting up and finally looking at me. "Mom left the invitation out for me this morning."

"Oh," I say. "I thought it was just girls." It's always

been just girls. A boy-girl pool party . . . why didn't Brianna say so?

Ronan stands up. "Well, I'll be there," he says, and then he starts to head back to his place.

"Where are you going now?" I ask him. Because I kind of thought the Transformer thing was an excuse to come over, to hang out with me for the day. I'm pretty bored, and Brianna is busy unpacking because they only just moved this week.

Ronan says, "Home." And that doesn't leave me much to work with.

I sit out on the porch and text Brianna. It takes forever to go through because Twin Pines is in a dead zone where the signal only works if the clouds are hanging just so in the sky, as my mom says. That's why we still have a regular phone too.

Claire: Your pool party is boy-girl?

Waiting. Watching. Wind blowing the long grass around Mrs. Gonzalez's trailer because she's older, and even though we have an every-now-and-then person who comes to mow, she's on the edge of the field and it grows really fast and wild there. I kind of like it wild though—she gets lots of those fluffy-seed dandelions you can blow in people's faces, and she doesn't mind if we pick them so Ronan and I can have Flower Wars. My bedroom window looks out on her yard, and I used to angle myself so I could only see her wild patches. I'd pretend I lived in the countryside, with tangled spots of flowers and long, arching grass.

Finally. A ding.

Brianna: yes! eden says it'll be better

Eden. That's Brianna's cousin who's visiting for the summer. I met her last year when she was in town for a few days. She's twelve, but a grade older, so almost thirteen.

I don't want to have a too-big reaction to the party news, so I just text back *cool*.

I kick off my dusty flip-flops and go inside, escaping the heat and thinking about maybe putting some tea bags into a pitcher for sun tea.

Mom will be happy when she gets back and finds her puzzle piece and a cold pitcher of sugary tea spread out like offerings on our folding table. She likes it when I'm "productive."

But first I go into my room and find the invitation that came in the mail yesterday. It's on the nightstand next to my bed, and I open it up carefully so I don't tear the shiny peach envelope. The paper inside is thick, almost like cardboard, and the writing is cursive and fancy.

You're invited to the twelfth birthday of
Miss Brianna Lane Foley
Saturday the 23rd of June
at 3 o'clock in the afternoon
415 Hobson Terrace
Bring your bathing suits!
Regrets only 555-4350

Now I'm starting to think Ronan came over just to brag about being invited! I wonder which other boys will be there.

And I wonder how often Brianna is talking to Eden, or when that started. I guess it makes sense to include boys now that we're going to be twelve. I don't have big birthday parties—it's usually just me, Mom, and Dad, but I realize that if friends were invited, those friends would include Ronan, so technically I'm a boy-girl party kind of person.

But still. A boy-girl pool party . . . why didn't Brianna tell me?

Chapter 2

Mom comes home late in the afternoon and I'm watching TV. "Clairebear!" Her voice is bright and I know it was a good day. "I brought you a new swimsuit!"

I stand up to give her a side hug. She smooths my hair as I lean into her soft T-shirt.

"Have a look," she says. "Tags and everything. The Skylers are going up to the lake through August, so Mrs. Skyler bought a bunch of suits. This one was a little too small for Gemma so . . . it's yours."

I pick up the two-piece suit with neon triangles on it. It's cute. Maybe not what I would choose, but definitely wearable. When I glance at the price tag, I know it must be a good brand even though I don't recognize the name. Gemma Skyler wouldn't get anything less. She's two years older than I am, and Mom's been cleaning the Skylers' house since we were kids. When we were really little Gemma and I would play together while Mom worked. Her tree house is bigger than my bedroom—we had a lot of fun there.

"Thanks, Mom," I say. Now I have a new bathing suit to wear to Brianna's party.

"You're welcome, baby."

"Oh! I have something for you too," I tell her, moving aside so she can see my welcoming table setup. "I made sun tea, and look what I found . . ." I pick up the blue-flowered puzzle piece and wave it in front of her eyes.

"The missing piece!" She grabs it and hurries over to the tray by the TV where she's kept the hydrangea puzzle, unfinished, for months. Mom fits the last piece in, and I see her body actually relax. She likes completion. She doesn't even blame me for losing the piece, and I'm glad.

"Where will you put this one?" I ask her. The walls in our hallway are already filled with framed puzzles.

"I'm thinking in the kitchen," she says. "When we look at it, it'll be like we have fresh flowers on the counter each day." Then she yawns, even though it's only four thirty in the afternoon. "Okay, Clairebear, I'm gonna take a shower."

While the water runs, I pour a glass of ice tea and sit on the couch with the catalog Mom brought in from the mailbox. Then there's a knock on our screen door.

It's Ronan. He's changed into a nice shirt.

"Hey," he says. "I need your help."

Ten minutes later, Ronan and I are standing at the top of the hill in Cleland Cemetery, which is the closest place nearby where my phone can get a solid signal. Ronan has an old flip phone that doesn't go online, so I'm his internet source when he can't use his family computer.

At first his face looked so serious that I got worried, but it turned out that he just wanted a good phone camera to take a picture of himself. So I yelled to Mom that I'd be back soon, and I walked out with him.

"What do you need this for, anyway?" I ask him. Then I get a suspicion. "Are you allowed to be on social media?" I'm not until I'm thirteen. Mom says that's when it's legal.

"Just take the picture, Claire," he says in response, so I snap him wearing his new-looking striped polo shirt and standing in front of the big old oak tree that makes a nice backdrop, as long as I don't get any of the gravestones in the bottom of the frame.

I glance at the image on my screen. Ronan looks older, like a teenager already, in his nice shirt. I notice that his jaw seems more grown-up, if a jaw can be such a thing. It's sharp angled and tough looking.

Ronan grabs the phone from me.

"That'll work." He forwards it to his email, and his face goes from serious to smiling when he says, "Wanna hit the brook?"

I nod. I've been waiting to get to the brook all day. It's nearly ninety-five degrees out.

Ronan starts running, and I'm on his heels; I've always been *almost* as fast as he is. He kicks off his fake

Crocs at the edge of the water, but I barrel on in with my flip-flops. "They're water shoes!" I say when he looks at me funny. "And so are yours."

He laughs. "I forgot!" he says, climbing into the green rubber shoes and then wading back out to me. There are tiny pebbles under the water, so shoes help.

We make our way to the big black rock just around the southern bend of the brook from the clearing where we entered. I think of it as our rock, mine and Ronan's, though I've never said that out loud.

I scramble up and settle myself on the butt-size ledge at the top while Ronan leans against the broad side of the rock and closes his eyes. There's something sad about the way he does it slowly, for the second time today, like he can't handle the daylight anymore.

"You should bring Ellie here with us sometime," I say. Ellie is Ronan's pet lizard. He got her when his dad left, I guess because his mom felt bad or something. I don't think a lizard replaces a dad, but Mom told me it isn't for me to say.

Ronan grins. He loves Ellie. He named her after our student teacher that year, Miss Ellie, who always let

Ronan sit by her side at morning meeting that spring when his dad went away.

"I taught her to flick out her tongue on command," he says.

"No way!"

"Yup. All I have to do is stick out my tongue and she does it back."

"Cool. I think Ellie is an uncharacteristically smart lizard."

"I like it when you use eight-syllable words," Ronan says.

Then we count *uncharacteristically* out on our hands, and he's right. Eight syllables.

We're quiet for a while, me sitting up high and Ronan standing, leaning with our rock against his back. Even though it feels still and humid where we are, there's a little breeze up high. It's working its way through the green leaves above me, making them twitch and dance.

"You know why I love this place?" Ronan asks.

"Why?"

"Because there's no them, there's just us," he says.